THE DEVIL'S SNARE

BOOK 15

CRAIG HALLORAN

Dragon Wars: The Devil's Snare - Book 15

By Craig Halloran

★★★★★

TWO-TEN BOOK PRESS

PO Box 4215, Charleston, WV 25364

ISBN eBook: 978-1-946218-94-0

ISBN Paperback: 979-8-711205-83-8

ISBN Hardback: 978-1-946218-95-7

www.dragonwarsbooks.com

Publisher's Note

This book is a work of fiction. Names, characters, places, and incidents either are the product of the author's imagination or are used fictitiously, and any resemblance to actual persons, living or dead, events, or locales is entirely coincidental.

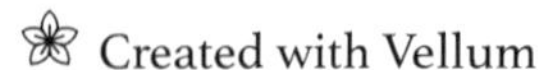

Gapoli
Ice Vale
Dark Mountain
Ugrad
Far Stick
Black Stow
Crack Scowl
Green Ridge
Agustun
Staatus
Loose Boot
Kenna
Dagger Ford
Inland Sea
Westerlund
Monarch City
Arrow Wood
Doverun
The Great River
Dortam
Harbor Lake
Raven Cliff
Iron Hills
Red Bone
Haalum
Ferry Lunn
Havenstock
Farhook
Sulter Slay
Willowacks
Valley Shire
Mortus
Debble Bolt
Salt Knob
Oldham
Hotvale
Gunder Island
Crow Valley
Dwarf Skull
The Shelf
Gold Hook
Littleton

1

THE PAST – WIZARD WATCH TOWER

The tip of the Rod of Weapons glowed with angry fire. Grey Cloak held it in a white-knuckled grip. Zanna Paydark stood holding her arms out between him and Gossamer.

"Get out of the way, Mother!" he growled in a low voice. "He betrayed us. You betrayed us. I won't let that happen again."

They were sealed inside the belly of the Wizard Watch tower, surrounded by a ring of stone walls and archways. A great fountain spouted water in the middle, where crystal-clear water trickled, gurgling like an outdoor stream.

"Grey Cloak, listen to me, please," Zanna pleaded. The elven natural flipped her silky black locks out of her face, and her long fingernails glowed with fire. She was an imposing woman, dressed in a black jerkin and trousers, with many blades strapped to her body that she could snag at any moment. "This was the only way." She motioned to Gossamer. "This is the past. Gossamer is not yet guilty of what he will do."

"I don't care." Grey Cloak marched forward. He pointed his weapon's tip in her face. "If I kill him now, he won't be able to betray us. Get out of the way."

Zanna eased her face away from the rod's burning tip. "If you kill him now, we'll all be doomed."

Gossamer stood far behind Zanna, wearing a curious expression. The elven wizard's half-black, half-white hair framed his face. He wore black-and-white-checkered robes and held a cane with a silver handle. "Zanna, would you care to tell me what's going on?"

"It's a long story that I'll never get to tell if you are dead," she stated.

"I see." Gossamer nodded. He peered over her shoulder at Grey Cloak and Dyphestive. "Hello, I'm Gossamer. It is a divine pleasure to meet you both."

"Gum up, you two-faced swine!" Grey Cloak said. "Move, Mother. I'm going to finish this."

"Perhaps we should hear them out before we shed any blood," Dyphestive suggested.

Grey Cloak turned his heated gaze toward Dyphestive. "I'd rather not. I'm tired of dealing with deceitful people and these towers."

Dyphestive leaned on his sword. He wore a sheepskin vest and buckskin trousers. He stared at Gossamer and

Zanna. "It's us against you. I stand by my brother. I'll offer a solution. If you want to talk, let us out so we can talk outside rather than be trapped inside this tower."

"We are only safe inside these walls," Zanna warned. "We need to remain within."

"I like the idea." The youthful Gossamer tapped his cane on the floor. One of the slabs behind the archway vanished, letting in warm sunlight.

Grey Cloak did a double take between the inside and the out. He started to back away. "I'll play."

Streak popped his head out of Grey Cloak's hood. "I'll play too."

"Dyphestive, get the horses. Make it quick." He kept his eyes on Zanna. "Are you coming or not?"

"You're making a mistake." She shook her head. The glow in her fingertips went out. "You have to trust me."

"No thanks. I'll take my chances elsewhere." He followed Dyphestive and the horses out of the tower and stood in an open field of flowers on a hot summer day. They stood among small, colorful trees. "Whoa. This isn't the same place as we entered. Where are the rocks?"

Zanna joined him outside, followed by Gossamer, who kept his distance. "We're southeast, below Littleton, near the Great River. Not many come here, but we are very far from the enemy that sought to pursue you."

Grey Cloak gazed warily at Zanna and Gossamer then the outer walls of the tower. The tall structure was covered in moss and ivy vines that decorated it in clumps. Birds nested in the nooks of the arches, and the tower listed slightly. The weathered facility, covered in nature, had the look of a great tree among the flowery fields. He dimmed the power in his rod. "Fair enough. Talk."

Zanna sighed. "We are still at risk here, but hopefully you will listen to reason."

"I'm all ears," he said.

She motioned for Gossamer. He approached, his robes dragging over the flowery grasses.

"I'm very eager to hear what you have to say," he said.

Grey Cloak kept his eyes glued to the young elven wizard. The two of them had battled fierce dragons to the death inside the tower. The beast had nearly killed them, but Gossamer had fought valiantly. That was why his betrayal came as such a surprise. Without warning, Gossamer had jettisoned Grey Cloak and Dyphestive through the Time Mural and into the past. "Speak, Zanna." He glanced up at the clear blue skies. "We don't have all day, apparently."

She raised a brow and nodded. A monarch butterfly with bright-green wings landed on her shoulder for a moment and took off again. "This won't be an easy matter for you to wrap your minds around, but I'll do my best to explain."

"We can only hope," he said.

"At this point in time, I think I have no choice but to opt

for full disclosure." Zanna adjusted one of the knives tucked inside her wrist bracers. "Gossamer is the one that sent me back in time to find you two."

It was Grey Cloak's turn to raise a brow. "Really? How convenient."

"Hear her out, brother. I'm intrigued," Dyphestive said.

"As am I." Gossamer moved closer to Zanna. "How can this be?"

"The fact that we're here is proof that it can be, but there is a grave risk of it all imploding." Her eyes met Grey Cloak's. "This is why I insisted we stay in the tower, but perhaps outside is best." She faced Gossamer. "This affects you most of all, and I shudder to think what might happen when I tell you what I know."

Gossamer put a hand on her shoulder. "I trust you as much as I trust Jerrik. Say what must be said."

2

"I DON'T CLAIM to understand everything I'm about to say. I will only share what I know," Zanna said with a heavy look. "Gossamer freed me in the future, not long after he sent Grey Cloak and Dyphestive through the portal. In the future, you serve Black Frost."

"I knew it!" Grey Cloak said. "And we're trusting him and you now?"

Zanna lifted her hand. "Hear me out, son, before your ears burn off. Gossamer acted as a spy. He set the entire matter up. Even before he betrayed you, he knew what he was doing, all because of this conversation. Let that sink in."

Streak's head tilted. "I get it."

Dyphestive wore a puzzled expression.

Grey Cloak thought out loud. "You're telling us that in

the future, Gossamer had to act according to what you're telling him now? So, he went through the motions all the way up to our betrayal? How is that possible?"

"It's possible because we're going to fill him in now on the role that he must adhere to. If he does not, or did not, we wouldn't be here at this very moment," Zanna said. "What that means is, Gossamer came through. He can be trusted."

"Forgive me if I don't leap for joy, but this could all be a lie."

"True, but it isn't," Zanna continued. "This is what Gossamer told me, and you can decide for yourself. In the future, after you're sent to the past, Gossamer destroys the portal. Black Frost tasks him to rebuild the Time Mural. The moment he does, he frees me from the stone and sends me back in time to find you."

"Why did he send us into the past?" Dyphestive asked.

"To keep you safe from Black Frost. It was the only way to hide you and buy time," she said.

Grey Cloak rubbed his temples. "This is a lot to soak in. It gives me a skull ache."

"And if you don't believe me, Gossamer told me to tell you about the hydra you battled in the dungeons. You fought and defeated it several times. If this is true, how could I have known that?" she asked.

"Clever. I have no idea how you could have known that." Grey Cloak huffed. "What do you think, brother?"

"It's certainly plausible."

Grey Cloak whispered to Dyphestive, "Maybe she can read my thoughts."

"I'm not reading your mind, and I have excellent hearing, you should know." Zanna sat down and plucked a flower. She picked off the petals one by one. "Do you believe me or not?"

"Give us a moment to think about it." Grey Cloak's wheels turned inside his head. "It's a great deal of fantastic information, but I don't follow how any of this is going to help us defeat Black Frost. If anything, matters are worse if he has access to the Time Mural. He'll be able to invade another world, won't he?"

"That's why we have to stop him in the past," she said. "Before he becomes too strong to kill, if that's even possible." She looked up at the sky and into the tower's opening. "We should really go inside."

"Not so fast." Grey Cloak raised a finger. "I have more questions. I find it hard to believe your escape from Dark Mountain was so simple. Certainly, your statue went missing. And how would you make it out of there, into the Wizard Watch, where the Time Mural is?"

Zanna picked another flower. "Gossamer has an ally named Datris."

"I know that name." Grey Cloak searched his memories. "He was an adept like me, at Hidemark—one of twelve elves. After Black Frost destroyed the Sky Riders, I never saw him again."

"He opted to serve Black Frost rather than be destroyed like the others. He felt his survival would be imperative to save our cause, and he gained Black Frost's trust." Zanna glanced at Gossamer. "According to you, Datris and I switched images. He made a sacrifice and turned to stone as me, while I assumed the identity of Datris using a transformation spell. It fooled Black Frost, well, at least long enough for me to escape through the rebuilt portal."

"Zooks, this tale gets taller and taller." Grey Cloak kicked the flowers. Zanna had filled in most of the gaps with a very convincing story, but he still resisted believing her entirely. "Brothers, do you believe this?"

"I buy it," Streak said. "It would be a fantastic movie."

Everyone gave him a funny look.

Gossamer adjusted his black-and-white robes and took a knee by Zanna. "I understand my responsibility. Tell me what I must know."

"Grey Cloak and Dyphestive will have to fill you in on the details," she said.

Grey Cloak sighed reluctantly. "You and Tatiana are imprisoned in the tower by the underlings from another world. You serve them, building the Time Mural, or making it better, for part of a decade. I can't say what happens inside there, but you'll have to aid them until Dyphestive and I arrive. It's not long after that when we battle the hydra, and you toss us back through the hole for a second time."

"I'm going to need more details," Gossamer said.

"Well, it seems we have plenty of time," he replied, "unless we try to put an end to Black Frost now. He won't see us coming." He looked at Zanna. "Surely you've seen something from the future that will destroy him."

"What I know will not be enough," she dryly said. "He feeds on another world, and we need to cut off that source of power from within. Finding a way to close that portal is no small matter. Gossamer in the future has looked into it, and the source flows like a river. It cannot be closed so easily, and not without destroying the world on the other side. Black Frost contains all its power."

"Can we kill him?" Dyphestive asked. "If we do, won't the energy flow back?"

"Kill him, hah." Zanna tossed the flower stem aside. "We don't even know how to harm him."

3

THE TENSION between Grey Cloak and Gossamer eased, and he filled the wizard in on every detail he could recall while Dyphestive and Zanna talked separately. "You're going to have to walk a tightrope to remember all of this."

"Remembering isn't the problem. Acting it out in sequence is. I'll do my best," the soft-spoken Gossamer said.

"I can't help but want to ask you questions about the future. It's easy to forget you haven't arrived there yet."

"Agreed. I feel the same way, but the less I know, the better." Gossamer polished the silver handle of his cane on his cloak. "I envy you in regards to time travel. I think that journey would be fascinating. You should consider it a blessing."

"I don't know about that. It's more of a curse. The

longer I live, the more my friends die." He leaned closer to Gossamer, hoping Zanna's keen ears wouldn't pick up his voice. "Don't you think it would be easier to stop Black Frost now?"

"Perhaps, but your father once said to me that when an enemy is at their strongest, they are also at their weakest," the mage replied.

"What does that mean?"

"I believe it's a reference to overconfidence, pride perhaps. Black Frost will be on his guard when he is young with power, but soon he will be so strong that he won't even worry about it." Gossamer shrugged his narrow shoulders. "That's why we should be patient and strike when he believes he has won."

Grey Cloak nodded. "That makes sense, but we might be missing a grand opportunity right now. Let me bounce a few ideas off you."

"How are you feeling, Festive?" Zanna asked. They stood beside the tower's wall, near the entrance. "We haven't had much time to get to know one another. Tell me what's on your mind."

"I'm worried. I've seen so many die, and I feel I'm at fault."

"Don't be foolish. Let me ask you this. Did your friends live doing what they wanted?"

"I think so," he said.

"Would you die the same for them as they died for you?"

"Certainly. I understand. But I've thought about that, and something's nagging inside me. I want to go back and save them, at any cost."

Zanna offered him a clever smile. She tucked his hair behind his ear. "You are your father. He felt the same way. Tell me, who is she?"

"Leena," he said with a shaky voice. "I never even got to say goodbye, and the next thing I knew, she was gone." His chin sank to his chest. He sobbed. "I miss her."

"There, there." Zanna embraced him the best her arms would allow. "I understand your pain. You have nothing to be ashamed of. We all feel this. If we didn't, we wouldn't fight for the ones we love." She broke away and placed her hand on his chest. "You have a big heart. It hurts, and you need time to mourn."

"So much has happened. I don't want to forget." He gave her a guilty look. "Sometimes I do."

"That's understandable and nothing we all don't go through. Life goes on, Dyphestive. That doesn't mean the ones who have moved on can't be a part of it." She took his hand and walked him around the tower. "You need to find a place, and a day, where you can remember your friends."

"Like a grave? I don't think she has one."

"Perhaps you can make a marker, in a beautiful place like this, and visit it from time to time." She tilted her head and faced him. "Would you like to tell me about her?"

"Uh." He nodded. "I would. She was a monk from the Ministry of Hoods. The first time I met her, she beat me up —well, in a way. She kept kicking me in the beans. I can still feel that."

Zanna giggled. "Go on."

"She had a long ponytail as dark as a raven's wings. Pretty eyes, but with a storm brewing in them. She didn't speak. She could be as frosty as a new snow, but I liked her, and she liked me." He rubbed his forehead with his meaty hands. "Is that strange? Loving a woman who doesn't talk?"

"Of course not. Actions speak louder than words. I'm sorry for your loss, Festive. But when the time comes, someone will fill that void." She squeezed his hands. "I know it. Come on, now. Let's go see what your brother is scheming. He doesn't trust me, does he?"

"He'll come around."

"I hope." She led the way to where Grey Cloak and Gossamer sat. "So, tell me, what grand scheme have you come up with to destroy Black Frost?"

"Who, us? I thought you had all the answers." Grey Cloak smirked. "And what makes you think we were scheming?"

"Because I know I would be." She squatted down beside

them. Streak crawled out of Grey Cloak's hood and lay at her feet. "Out with it. I know you're planning something."

"We started to, when another question came to mind," Gossamer said.

"Oh, and what is that?" she asked.

"Why did Black Frost build another Time Mural?" Gossamer asked.

"We understand he wants to open another world," Grey Cloak stated, "but he did that already. He could do it again, but you said he wants another Time Mural. That would only pose a greater danger to him, wouldn't you think?"

Zanna nodded. "That's a good question. Lucky for you, future Gossamer provided the answer."

4

ZANNA CONTINUED. "Gossamer and Datris told me that the Time Mural demands a lot more energy to move back and forth in time. The more energy, the farther it can go. Black Frost wants to go far enough back where he can destroy all of his enemies before they're a threat—farther back than this, even. He wants to make sure none of us ever exists, and he needs the Time Mural to do that. We pose the only threat to him."

"All the more reason to stop him now, in the past, before he can execute his plan," Grey Cloak said.

"Or us?" added Dyphestive.

"We have no easy answers," Zanna stated. "But I don't feel you're ready yet. You need more help and more time. We need to use the time while we have it." She stroked Streak's wings.

His twin tails curled.

"Now is the time for patience and planning. It's our best hope to defeat him." She looked Grey Cloak in the eye. "You are the best hope to defeat him." She eyed Dyphestive. "As well as you."

"No pressure there," Grey Cloak said. "But waiting around for a decade while we know that our friends are going to die, again?" He shook his head. "I can't think it, and I'm not going back in that tower. Besides"—he thumbed over his shoulder—"doesn't Black Frost have allies in there?"

"The wizards that roam the towers are very discreet. They keep to themselves unless bothered, which they don't like. And they don't have any reason to be searching for you," Gossamer said.

"Not that we know of." Grey Cloak paced the floral ground. He glanced at his brother.

Dyphestive shrugged his heavy brows.

"I think we need to stay outside. Certainly, we can find another discreet abode where you can prepare us, Zanna."

She gave him a doubtful look. "We would risk too much. A chance encounter with your friends is far too hazardous. And if you were to encounter yourselves, that would be fatal."

Grey Cloak snapped his fingers. "No, it won't because Dyphestive, Streak, and I were sent into the future. We won't be able to run into ourselves, at least not for a long time."

"You can't help but squirm out of this, can you?" Zanna's frown deepened. She stopped stroking Streak's wings and stood. "Fine. We'll try it your way, for now, but if we see a hint of danger, we must retreat to the towers. No questions asked. Bear in mind, Black Frost's forces are still searching for you everywhere."

Grey Cloak smirked. "Then I guess we'll have to come up with a really good disguise."

Dyphestive's face brightened. "So, we stay in the open." He took in a deep breath of fresh air. "I like it."

"We're near Littleton, a small mining town. The people are simple folk, who ask few questions," Gossamer said. "I would stick out like a thorn, but you shouldn't have much trouble blending in. It would be an excellent place for sanctuary."

"We won't be going into town, not unless we need special supplies. We will train and live off the land," she said.

With a long face, Dyphestive said, "What, no hot biscuits and gravy? Small towns make the best."

"It's nuts and berries for you, big fella. Of course, if you stay in the tower, you'll be able to eat whatever manner of food you desire," Zanna said.

Dyphestive gave Grey Cloak a pleading look. "Are you sure you don't want to go in the tower?"

"Have you ever eaten food in the tower?" asked Grey Cloak.

"No."

"Then what makes you think the food will be any better?"

Dyphestive nodded and rubbed his stomach. "I see your point."

Zanna shook hands with Gossamer. "I'm sorry for the burden we've placed on you."

"Don't be. I am honored." Gossamer squeezed her hand and looked at the brothers. "I won't fail you." He handed Zanna an amulet with a yellow tiger's-eye stone in it. "If you need sanctuary in the towers, use this. I'll be waiting." He waved his cane, turned his back, and walked through the tower's archway. The stone wall sealed behind him.

Zanna climbed into her horse's saddle and tucked the tiger's-eye amulet in a saddlebag. "Well, you got what you wished for. Saddle up. We have a new home to build, and you're going to hate it."

Grey Cloak and Dyphestive mounted and followed Zanna. Streak took flight.

Riding side by side with Dyphestive, Grey Cloak asked, "Do you think this is the right decision?"

Dyphestive shrugged his broad shoulders. "Who can tell? But I certainly prefer the open air with the wind in my face. As for feeding on varmints and venison for years, that I'm not so sure about."

"Neither am I." Grey Cloak looked over his shoulder. The tower faded into the landscape, and he was glad of it. He'd learned his lesson so far as the towers were concerned. They were trouble. Yet, his father, Jerrik, had served the Wizard Watch. It left him puzzled that his father could work among a group of people that were so mistrusted.

Tatiana and Dalsay aren't so bad. I suppose Gossamer isn't. But they're the few out of many.

He had enough weight on his shoulders. The fate of the world was at stake, and it was up to them to save it.

"Brother, what do you think about going after Black Frost now?" he asked.

"It's a bold thought without a plan, but I believe we should still keep thinking on it. It might not be the time to strike now, but who knows what opportunity might present itself a few months or a few years from now?"

"Exactly!" Grey Cloak said.

Zanna, who rode well ahead of them, turned her head for a moment and looked back.

Grey Cloak said, "I need to remember to keep my voice down."

5

STREAK SAILED high in the sky with his wings spread wide. He spotted a flock of wild geese, sped up, and zoomed through their ranks. The geese angrily honked a few times. White feathers floated toward the earth. They resumed their formation.

With a snigger, Streak barrel-rolled a few times and did a few loop the loops. He loved little more than flying, and in the vast wide open, he could be as big or small as he wanted. "Ah, the sweet taste of summer air. How it tickles the senses." He flicked his pink tongue out of his mouth and dove.

Below him were beautiful fields of tall grass and wild-flowers, groves of spring trees, and small bush-laden forests. He spotted varmints like jackrabbits and such huddled in the grasses. Deer and their fawns lay in bright flower beds. For a dragon, small or large, it was a smorgasbord.

Streak salivated. He dove.

A jackrabbit fled and zigzagged side to side.

Quick. Streak closed in. *But not quick enough.* He anticipated the rabbit's next move.

It zigged.

He zigged too.

Chomp!

Streak locked his jaws around the twitching jackrabbit and crushed the life from its limbs. He landed in a meadow and finished his meal. He burped out a furball. "That should tide me over. I better check on the others." He spread his wings and launched into the sky.

Even at a full gallop, the horses and riders were no match for Streak's speed. He flew as fast as any bird or dragon, and it became boring waiting for the others. He covered more ground and had a fantastic bird's-eye view of any danger ahead. It made him a perfect scout.

"It's good to be me—strong, fiery, fast, handsome, smart."

A wink of light caught his eye. It came from within a cluster of rocks, trees, and bushes stretched out like a scar upon the land.

He circled the area.

The bright sliver of light shined again and vanished.

"Hmmm… that was pretty. I better investigate." Streak

glided down toward the rocky landscape, keen eyes searching the spot where he saw the last flash.

The forest was rich in rock formations and deep crevices. Trees sprouted up along the ledges and leaned over the gorge. The closer he came to the out-of-place land, the more massive he realized it was.

A flash came and went from another spot.

Streak sped toward the area and landed on a small cliff that overlooked a deep black gorge cutting through the rocks like a snake. He dropped his head over the rim, his earholes on full alert.

From the darkness, light flashed again. It came from a ledge on the other side of the chasm only thirty feet down.

"Ah-ha." Streak flicked his tongue. His spikes stood on end.

Deep in the vein of the gorge, something moved. It scraped along the rocks far below him and fell silent. His head tilted side to side like a bird's. The air began to prickle. Light winked again. The fire burned brighter this time and stayed.

"Will you look at that?"

The light he'd spotted moments earlier burned on the ledge like a beautiful rose petal. It quavered with a welcoming glow. Inside the fire, a rose-colored gem sparkled like the coming dawn.

Streak lost his breath. His eyes grew. "I'm coming, darling." He spread his wings and dove into the gorge.

The rose fire went out. Darkness swallowed the runt dragon whole.

"Training. Every day?" Grey Cloak asked Zanna. "You can't be serious. We can't have that much more to learn."

Zanna slowed her horse and let Grey Cloak and Dyphestive catch up. "You need to be fully prepared for anything. Training will serve to hone the skills you already have and make them stronger. When dealing with your enemies, you need to dispatch them quickly."

"I thought we handled the Scourge rather well. When we first encountered them, they outmatched us." Dyphestive swatted at a fly buzzing around his horse's ear. "This time, we bested them."

Zanna huffed a laugh. "They never should have overmatched you the first time. You're naturals. They're no more than gnats."

The brothers shared a perplexed look.

"You make it sound like we're giants," Grey Cloak said.

"That's because you are. It's time you thought like one. You must have full confidence in your abilities," she stated.

"I told you I was trained by the Sky Riders. Dyphestive was trained by the Doom Riders. There is no better training than that. We're ready. We wouldn't have made it this far if we weren't," he said.

Zanna didn't even look at them as she laughed. "That was for a short time. You've both barely seen twenty seasons of life. I've trained daily for twenty seasons. That's the difference." Her gaze slid over to Dyphestive. "Look at you. You swat at the fly like a clumsy ox. You should be able to capture it in your fingertips."

"Look at him. He's built like an anvil," Grey Cloak said. "But I can catch that fly, no problem."

"That makes no difference," she said.

Dyphestive tried to grab the fly with his hand. He missed over and over again. "I can see her point. I should be able to grab a fly."

"With your fingertips," she insisted.

Dyphestive kept at it. "Think of Anya, brother. While we were gone, she went into hiding the entire time. All she did was train, and I think she got much better."

Grey Cloak dropped his head and sighed. "You would opt for more training, a glutton for punishment. You miss Rhonna's farm too much. The more backbreaking work, the better, in your mind."

"I do miss the farm life." Dyphestive gave a stiff nod. "It was fun."

"Listen, Zanna, I don't mind training, but I'm not going to spend all of my days doing it. We need to investigate Black Frost. Besides, in my book, experience is the best teacher."

"I'll tell you what." Zanna dismounted. "We'll spar. If

you defeat me, we do it your way, and if I win, we do it my way."

"Not this again." He recalled his battle with Anya for leadership of the Sky Riders. It had been nothing short of fierce. A cold sensation flooded his veins, and his arm hairs stood on end. He rose up in his saddle. "It will have to wait."

"Why?" she asked.

"Something's wrong with Streak." He dug his heels into his horse.

It jumped into a gallop.

He yelled, "Yah!"

6

GREY CLOAK PULLED his horse to a halt. His heart pounded inside his temples. He hadn't seen Streak in hours, which wasn't out of the ordinary, but he knew something was wrong. They had a special connection, and he tingled all over as he stared at an odd rupture in the middle of the flowery grasslands. "Streak, where are you?" he muttered.

Dyphestive and Zanna caught up with him and stopped by his side.

"What is that?" Dyphestive exclaimed. "It looks like the earth exploded and created an ugly forest."

"I don't know, but Streak is in there somewhere." Grey Cloak scanned what appeared to be miles of strange, naturally molested land. "But I've never seen a place like this." He glanced at his mother.

"Don't assume because I'm older I've seen everything either," she said.

"Of course not. You've been too busy training." Grey Cloak gave his horse a small kick and started toward the odd forest that looked like a mountain bursting from the ground.

Zanna rode her horse in front of him. "Where do you think you're going?"

"In there—or in that."

"What makes you think he's in there? He could be anywhere. Perhaps Streak will return soon, and we should wait."

"No, he's in there. I can feel him." Grey Cloak started leading his horse around her, but Zanna grabbed the reins. "Goy! Let go."

There was no mistaking her displeasure. "This never would have happened if we'd stayed in the tower. It's only been a day, and already, we've found trouble."

He jerked the reins out of her grip. "No worse trouble than what I've discovered in the towers. You don't have to come along. Stay here if you wish, but I'm going in." He rode for the gap in the rocky woodland filled with slate hill-tops, ledges, and spires. "Come on, Dyphestive."

Shoulders back and chin up, Dyphestive nodded at Zanna. "Streak is family. You should know that."

"Of course I know that. Oh, never mind." Zanna followed the brothers into the forest.

The rugged terrain was unlike any Grey Cloak had ever seen. Rocks rose where trees should have been, and trees stood where rocks should have been, growing all around them. Branches dangled over sloped hillsides. Seams between the rocks and trees made tight pathways. Birds fluttered in the branches but didn't chirp. Aside from the snorting horses and jangling of equipment, the place was as silent as a spotted deer.

"I have to be honest. I haven't chased down many dragons before, let alone a small one," Zanna admitted. "Do you have any idea what might have happened to him?"

Grey Cloak gave her an aggravated look. "No. But we'll find some sign if something happened to him here. Keep your eyes open and mouth closed, if you don't mind."

"We'll find him, brother," Dyphestive said.

The forest's strange layout would be the perfect hiding spot for all sorts of inhabitants. The huge rock formations and towering trees provided the perfect shelter as well. Any sort of creature could lurk in the dark crevices, oversized knotholes, and high branches. Grey Cloak didn't see any sign of anything, but the muscles between his shoulders remained tight.

He entered a dark channel between the rocks. It was black inside, with fountains of light peeking out in the distance. Staring deep inside, he asked, "What do you think?"

"It looks like the perfect place for evil to hide," Zanna said.

"Excellent. Perhaps we'll come across some old friends of yours," he said. "I'll lead the way."

The hollow passage snaked and twisted through the rocks and bases of petrified trees. They traveled over an hour without hearing a sound. When the wind picked up, it whistled sharply and howled moans. Daylight slipped from the sky, but its illumination died on the ledges.

A rotten odor wafted through the passage. The smell worsened the farther they went.

Grey Cloak crinkled his nose and covered it in his cloak. "What in the Flaming Fence is that scent? It's awful."

"That is the stench of death. It can be no other." Zanna covered her nose with her hand. "One never gets used to it."

"It doesn't bother me so much," Dyphestive commented. "It reminds me of the Dragon Kennels."

"The Kennels didn't smell like this," replied Grey Cloak. "We'll keep going as far as we can stand it. Something is eating something down here, and it better not be my dragon."

The passage wound downward in a long, gentle slope and turned like pretzel knots.

Grey Cloak's eyes watered. "Ew, this is getting bad. It smells like something crawled in one end of a dragon and came out the other, then did it all over again."

Zanna wiped her eyes. "If trouble's to be found, we will certainly find it here."

They came upon a massive bowl-shaped pit carved from a rock bed. It spanned the length of twenty horses and stood half as deep. It was filled with bones and rotting flesh of tremendous beasts.

"What in the world dragged those carcasses down here?" Grey Cloak asked.

His horse whinnied shrilly. Something moved among the dead flesh and bones. The horses bucked and snorted.

Grey Cloak fought against the reins. "Something moves! We need to get away from here!"

Vine-like tongues snaked out of the pit's mouth, latched onto the horses' legs, and dragged them in.

7

Before Grey Cloak could breathe another word, his horse was tangled in prickly vines and hauled into the pit, taking him with it. They hit the ground full force. The bones in the horse's hips cracked. It lay limp and wide-eyed. Grey Cloak scrambled away from the tendrils like a crab and braced his back against the wall. In horror, he watched the vines drag his horse into a deeper gap surrounded by bones.

Twisting and wriggling, tendrils came right at him. He fed wizard fire into the Rod of Weapons and formed the head of a scythe-like blade. He turned his hips in a vicious swing and cut clean through three hideous tendrils. A cry caught his ear.

"Aaaaaaargh!"

The living vines swallowed Dyphestive's horse.

He stood in the pit with the fierce growth twisting around his legs and waist. He attacked with the Iron Sword. His great arms chopped up and down, turning the clipped tendrils into goo. "Grey, what is this thing? It's everywhere!"

Grey Cloak danced between the vines that quickly slunk toward his legs like snakes. In a scooping swing, he sliced through the tendrils in a continuous motion. The cut tendrils coiled back into their hole. For every one hit, two more burst out of the hole.

Grey Cloak hacked away. "I don't know what it is, but we need to get out of here!"

"Agreed! *Umph!*"

A living vine wrapped around Dyphestive's mouth.

His wide eyes filled with shock then suddenly knitted together. He growled like a wild animal and crushed the tendrils in his jaws. "Grrrrrrrr!" He bit clean through it and spit the nasty tendril out. "Blech! Don't eat those things!" The muscles bulged in his arms, and he brought his sword down like a blacksmith's hammer. Gory monster splatter went everywhere.

A tendril slipped through Grey Cloak's defenses, wrapped around his ankle, and jerked him off of his feet.

"Zooks!"

The appendage was strong, like a wild beast. It towed him through the graveyard of rotten flesh and bones toward the hole. He raised up the rod and prepared to smite the vine. More tendrils seized his wrists in a snare. He struggled to pull free as his body slid closer to the hole. The tendrils were everywhere.

"Noooooo!" Grey Cloak cried.

Dyphestive appeared, hacking into the nasty tendrils. The living vines snaked around his mighty limbs. He would not be denied. His fierce chops were guided by the muscles in his unrelenting arms, which burst free of the barbed coils, ripping open the skin on his arms.

"Aaaaaagh!"

Dyphestive's mighty efforts were muted by a second surge of tendrils that consumed both brothers. His iron-strong limbs were seized as the vines wrapped him in a cocoon. Even he couldn't move.

Zanna appeared out of nowhere. She lingered over Grey Cloak with a soft, radiant glow coating her body. "May I borrow this?" She pried the Rod of Weapons from his fingers. He nodded. "Don't go anywhere. I shall return shortly. Hopefully."

Grey Cloak managed to sit up.

Zanna fed fire into the tip of the rod and leapt feetfirst into the black hole. Bright flashes of light erupted out of the hole, followed by inhuman shrieking. The tendrils flexed and squeezed. Thorns bit deep into flesh.

"Aauuuugh!" Grey Cloak yelled. "What is she doing, feeding it?"

A thunderous *boooooom* erupted from the hole. It spit hunks of flesh out like a fountain of doom. The strength in the suffocating tendrils faded. The living vines sagged.

Grey Cloak peeled his way out of the tendrils while Dyphestive kicked and tore through his own. Many slack tendrils slid back into the hole.

"Plah!" Grey Cloak spit foul grit from his mouth. He crawled through the slime toward the rim of the hole and peered down. He saw a small, smoldering glow deep in the hole. "Zanna?"

Her voice echoed. "Good guess. What was your first clue?"

"The stink."

"Funny," she replied. "The lurker is dead, but the stench will linger a lifetime. Come down."

Dyphestive leaned over the rim. "Is that Zanna?"

"No, it's the lurker."

"What's a lurker?"

"That thing we killed," Grey Cloak stated.

Zanna cleared her throat. "Ahem. That thing *I* killed. The pair of you were only feeding it."

"I would have thought of something." Grey Cloak jumped into the hole.

His cloak billowed out, and he floated to the bottom. His feet landed on the outline of a sharp ring of teeth that made up a mouth huge enough to swallow an entire horse or two. The lurker's body was a huge oval bulge of flesh with tendrils spooling out of it like yarn.

"Thunderbolts, this smells ghastly. How'd you kill it?"

Zanna poked the rod inside the lurker's jaws. "That clump of meat is the heart. I gored it... several times. It's the only way to kill a lurker." She plucked fleshy grit from her hair and face. "You would have known that if you were fully trained in Hidemark."

"I might have slept during some of those sessions." He shrugged. "But I would have thought of something."

"Of course." She tossed him the rod.

"Thanks."

The Iron Sword dropped from above and stuck in the ground between them.

Dyphestive shimmied down the tendrils lodged into the walls of the hole. He jumped the last few feet and started plucking thorns from his hands. He peered around. "What is this place?"

"If I didn't know better, I'd say it was an ogre's outhouse." Grey Cloak increased the rod's flame, illuminating the room.

The seam in the earth branched out into natural passages. Trails of bones and flesh littered the ground.

"I hope they don't all stink. Do you think there are more lurkers?"

Zanna shook her head. "I think that one is a guardian, used to lure in prey. They're crafty creatures known to even fool dragons. They make their own bait, the same as fishing, but fishing for warm flesh."

Grey Cloak's stomach sank. "If that's a guardian, then what is it guarding?"

"There's only one way to find out." Zanna pointed down the passage. "Would you like me to go first this time?"

8

THE PRESENT

RAZOR RETCHED over the side of the merchant ship. He'd been fine the first day of the trip up the Great River, but woke the next day with his stomach upside down. "Rusty nails, I feel like I drank swamp water." He wiped his mouth, turned green, and heaved over the side of the ship again. Once he finished, he sank into his seat. "Whose idea was this? I'd rather be riding a dragon."

"Drink this." Bowbreaker handed him a bucket of fresh water. The tall elven ranger had a physique like polished marble. His skin had a healthy brown tan, and his face was as expressionless as ever. "It will settle your belly."

Razor drank from the bucket. "Ah." He took another drink, swashed the water in his mouth, rose, and spit over the side. "Why don't you see if Captain Luhey will part with a bottle or two of wine? That will settle my stomach more than anything."

Bowbreaker pushed the bucket to his friend's lips. "Drink fully. We have a long journey. The sooner you get your legs, the better."

"Oh, my legs will be fine." Razor gulped a few more swallows. "As fine as monarch wine."

Talon had purchased passage on a merchant ship sailing north from a small port city leagues above Littleton. The vessel's main mast caught the river wind, which filled the swelling white sail. The craft rode north through the surging river waters, bumping them up and down. Captain Luhey, a squat part-orcen man with watery eyes and a patchy beard, had explained that there had been heavy storms in the north, causing the surge in the Great River. Captain Luhey's crew comprised ten men, plus the members of Talon, which included Zora, Tatiana, and Gorva along with Razor and Bowbreaker.

Anya journeyed in the sky, keeping a lookout with Cinder and some of his children. Their mission was simple —recover the Dragon Helm from behind the Flaming Fence.

Zora joined the men while Tatiana and Gorva spent time with the captain at the ship's bow.

"How are you feeling, Razor?" she asked.

With the sun in his eyes, he looked upon her shapely figure. "Better now that you arrived."

"Even with a green face, you're still a hound," Zora replied as she took a seat beside him.

Razor howled. "Awhooo! Can you blame me? I melt when I look into those eyes as bright as emeralds."

She shoved her shoulder into him. "You melt when any woman walks by."

"That's not true. I only have eyes for you."

"Uh-huh. I overheard you say the same thing to Gorva yesterday."

Razor managed a charming smile. "I don't think I used those exact words."

"No, because she has brown eyes, brown like—" She tilted her head. "How did you put it?"

"As brown as chestnuts."

Zora giggled. "It's no wonder she walked away."

"Yes, but this ship is too small. She has nowhere to go. I'll corner her later, when I can stand again."

Bowbreaker propped his foot up on the ship's rail. His dark eyes were distant as he studied the land on the starboard side of the ship. "It's going to be a long journey if Razor can't corral his tongue."

Razor looked up at the elven warrior. "If you weren't as rigid as a shipboard, you might find a way to enjoy yourself."

"Our mission is grave. This is no time to jest," replied Bowbreaker. "We need to focus."

"I'll focus on what I want between here and there. You

focus on what you want. These could be our last days together. We should enjoy them."

Bowbreaker dropped his foot and walked away.

"Say, you forgot your bucket!" Razor scratched the scruff on his neck. He leaned his head toward Zora. "What do you see in that elf? This bucket is more friendly than he is."

"I don't see anything in him."

Razor lifted his eyes. "Sure you don't. I see the way you look at him. And shame on you, using me to make him jealous."

"Uh! I did no such thing!"

"You can't fool me." He tapped his chest. "I know the game better than anyone."

Zora's cheeks flushed.

He pointed at her. "See? Aha!" He squeezed her knee. "It's good though."

"What's good?"

"Not feeling like you're dead inside. You have something to live for. We all do."

"You really don't think about where we're going, do you?"

Razor leaned his head back. "No sense in worrying about it until we get there. That won't change a thing."

"You do know we're going to the Flaming Fence, right?"

"I try not to think about it." He slid his gaze over to Tatiana. "I only hope that she knows what she's talking about, because if she doesn't, she's going to get us all killed."

"Do you trust her?"

"I've been with her a long time. I trust her. Do you?"

Zora nodded.

"That's all the affirmation I need." Razor sat up in his seat and craned his neck around. "Where'd the captain go?"

"Below deck. Why?"

"Why don't you see if you can talk him out of a bottle or three? I don't think he likes me."

"I can't imagine why." Zora put her hand on his shoulder and pushed up. "I'll see what I can do."

He watched her cute little walk until she vanished below deck. "The Flaming Fence." He drank again from the bucket and sighed. "Lords of the Air. We're dead and too stupid to know it."

9

A STAR-FILLED blanket of black loomed above on a moonless night. Zora sat wrapped up in a blanket on the small poop deck at the stern of the ship. Her eyes searched the deep waters, where small, glowing fish swam and jumped in the ship's surge. She'd seen many small wonders in the vast river that widened nearly a league in some places. She brushed a lock of auburn hair from her eyes and thought about Grey Cloak and Dyphestive.

I miss them.

The blood brothers she'd grown so fond of were lost. She could only pray they returned, somehow. Talon wasn't the same without them. She would never forget the first time she met them, young and naïve, and she'd stolen a dagger from them, among other things. They'd tracked her down, and in an unusual twist of events, they'd turned the tables.

"A talent for your thoughts," Tatiana said. The beautiful elven sorceress sat down beside Zora. The river breeze tussled the silky locks of her gorgeous hair. She managed a smile, but hard lines that didn't use to be there formed in the corners of her eyes. She searched the sky. "Well?"

"I was thinking about Grey Cloak and Dyphestive. Do you think we'll see them again?" Zora asked.

"There's no one else I'd rather see. I miss them too. But Gossamer could have sent them anywhere. His deception I did not see." Tatiana frowned. "You think you know somebody. Listen, without a Time Mural, or Gossamer, we can't bring them back. All we can do is continue the quest, the same as we've always done."

"Yes, well, we're doing that. But there are so few of us left. I never imagined it would be like this when I started. It was me, you, Dalsay, Adanadel, Browning, and Tanlin. Lords, Tanlin. I hope he is well. I miss him too."

"Tanlin can take care of himself. I'm certain of that."

"I wish I could see him again." Her eyes drifted to Gorva and Razor, who were rolling dice with some of the crewmen on the ship. "Even though I have a new family, I still feel very alone."

Tatiana put her long arm over the half-elf woman's shoulders. "You'll always have me, little sister. I promise."

"Promise me you won't jump through any portals."

"I can't promise that. After all, we have one more to go through."

A chill ran down Zora's spine. "Are you talking about the Flaming Fence?"

Tatiana nodded.

"Have you ever considered that the Dragon Helm is safe where it is? Perhaps it was put there for a reason."

"I have thought about that. It's consumed my thoughts." Tatiana leaned back against the wall of the stern and crossed her legs. "But creating the Dragon Helm was the initial mission. It was everything we strove for. If we can gain control of the dragons, we can turn the tide against Black Frost."

"It's as simple as that?"

"It's our only hope."

"I hate to ask, but I'm not like Razor. I worry. Will you tell me more about the Flaming Fence? Is it truly real?"

Tatiana nodded. "It is. It resides in the bowels of the mountains above Far Stick. At least, that's the only entrance we know of. Many believe it's a place where the dead go after they die, but it is real. It's a place where demons dwell. The fence is what keeps them from escaping."

Zora swallowed. She'd only heard demons mentioned a few times in her lifetime. Like the Flaming Fence, the comments carried a certain gravity. "What are these demons?"

"Long before time as we know it, Gapoli was ruled by

dragons, giants, and men, who lived in harmony. After eons of a peaceful coexistence, the Time of Trouble came. Self-centered leaders rose on all sides. They teamed up and waged war for dominion over all. According to the ancient lore, the evil leaders were hunted down and trapped in the bowels of the land. The forces of good prevailed and locked them behind the Flaming Fence. No one has seen the demons since."

Tatiana's dreaded words felt like a great weight on Zora's shoulders. She had no desire to visit such a place. "If they can't escape, how can we enter?"

"The Flaming Fence was created to keep their kind—the wicked, the depraved—within." Tatiana gave Zora a grave look. "So long as our intentions are pure, we should be able to escape."

"And how do we know our intentions are pure?"

"We'll find out when we try to escape ourselves."

The crew members stirred. They moved across the ship's floor and pointed at the distant lanterns of an approaching ship.

Zora and Tatiana joined Captain Luhey. The bowlegged sailor smoked a cigar and held the wheel steady.

"What's going on?" Zora asked.

"See that ship? Those blue flames in the lanterns are elven. Now that we've passed Mortus, they consider this part of the river their territory, same as I told you when we departed." He gave the wheel a quarter turn. "If I know the captain, we won't have much of a hassle, but don't take any chances. Your party needs to grease up and get behind the oars. Blend in with my crew. With any fortune, they won't board. But if they do, they check the cargo through and through." He huffed out a big yellow ring of smoke. "Don't worry. I can handle this. Get moving. They'll be here before you know it."

10

"PSST! WHERE'S BOWBREAKER?" Zora asked Razor. She and the other members of Talon had stripped down into dirty long shirts, messed up their hair, marred their faces with dirt and grease, and manned benches behind the oars.

"How should I know? I don't watch his every move. I should be asking you," Razor responded.

"Will you keep your voices down? I'm trying to hear them talk," Gorva said with one side of her head tilted up. She sat beside Zora in the row behind Razor and Tatiana. Four other crew members joined them on the other side.

They dropped their anchor, and the merchant ship came to a stop. The elven ship bumped alongside them, and they heard the footsteps of many soldiers walking on the deck above.

Razor looked at the roof above him. "How many elves

does it take to search a ship? There must be a score of them up there."

"Hush!" Gorva whispered.

The murmur of quiet conversation carried down the stairs leading topside. Before long, footsteps echoed down the stairs. More than one level stood above the shallow oar room used for guiding the ship into docks and bays. Barrels scraped against the floor. Wooden crates were lifted and dropped. The tiny deckhand quarters sounded as if they were being thoroughly searched. Before long, the search party of elven sailors made their way into the room where the oarsmen waited.

Zora stooped over, and her messy hair covered her eyes. She still managed a glimpse between Razor and Tatiana's shoulders. The graceful elves eased into the room, keeping their necks bent to avoid the beams. Three in all, they wore dark jerkins with leather chest cords. Their leather sword belts carried sabers and curved knives. Their elegant features formed masks of concentration as their gazes bore into the oarsmen.

Captain Luhey ambled in behind them. The boards groaned beneath his girth. He carried a lantern in the dim light and was sweating all over. He cleared his throat. "This is what's left of the ship, Captain Cravvit. Many of my crew use this room for sleeping. We're a little crowded, as I've taken on new hands."

"I can see for myself," the leader of the elven sailors

said in a controlled leathery voice. His shoulder-length locks were stringy and gray. He was dressed from head to toe in black, with shiny leather corsair boots. “This is a large crew for a small ship.”

Razor sat closest to him on the inside of the aisle.

The elf squeezed his shoulder. “This one is beefy. Are you going to sell him?”

“A strong back like that? No, I don’t have plans to. He’s a free man. I can use him.”

“Is that so?” Captain Cravvit grabbed Gorva’s chin. “What about this one? I could use a hand like this.”

“Again, she’s a free woman. Works on the ship. I have a few crewmen that will depart at Green Ridge, and these are the replacements. I’ll need them for the trip.”

Captain Cravvit huffed. “You don’t need anyone to pull oars to bring you downriver.”

“No, but I need them to guide me into the docks and help unload,” Luhey responded. “It’s difficult to find good workers these days.”

“Hmm...” Captain Cravvit moved in front of Tatiana. She kept her eyes averted. He pulled her face toward him. “And what does this beauty do? I’ve never seen a sailor with such looks before.” He grabbed her hands and checked them. “No calluses here. These palms are as soft as a newborn.”

Luhey gulped. “She’s a special passenger.” His arm holding the lantern trembled. “Going to Far Stick. Paid extra for passage. I don't ask questions when the gold shines like lanterns."

Captain Cravvit slowly spun around and poked Luhey in the belly. "This better not be a slave ship, Captain Luhey. I don't know you personally, but I know your past. You begin trading flesh, and we'll sink your ship like a stone."

"No, no, it's no such thing. I swear it," Luhey stammered. "I hold no records for slave trade. You can search. Captain Muushen will vouch for me. Certainly, you know him. I'm an honest merchant now."

"There's no such thing as an honest merchant." Captain Cravvit looked back at Zora. "Did that one pay for passage too?"

"No, she's a hand—quick on the deck and good for climbing the ropes."

Captain Cravvit turned away. He shoved by the captain. "Get your story straight, Captain Luhey. You'll likely encounter more searches along the way."

Luhey rubbed the back of his head. "Perhaps that's why we haven't seen as many ships on this trip. Er… might I ask why?"

"Queen Esmarelda searches for one, a wild elf called Bowbreaker. She's obsessed with him."

"I see. Pardon, but what does he look like?"

"An obsidian-haired elf among elves." Captain made a razor-thin smile. "If my hair were so black, I'd swear the elf was me." He hollered up top. "Sailors! It's time to abandon this wreck!"

The elven sailors departed. Their ship unhitched from the merchant vessel and resumed its journey downriver.

Everyone headed back up on deck. They found Bowbreaker standing on the stern, dripping wet.

"Huh," Captain Luhey said. "So you're the elf they're looking for. Don't worry. You're safe on my ship with my crew. This isn't the first time Queen Esmarelda's searched for something I have." He grinned proudly. "I'm really good at this." He kicked a plank near the poop deck. A small, concealed hatch opened up. "Grab your gear. You never know when you might need it."

11

"THERE SHE IS!" Captain Luhey said. "The gates to the Elven Basin." He stood behind the wheel while the members of Talon gathered at the ship's bow. "Gorgeous, isn't it?"

Zora marveled. "I've never seen statues so big."

The river's neck widened into a basin so large they couldn't see from one side to the other, transforming into an inland sea of clear blue waters. A tremendous bridge supported by stonework pillars rose high above the ship's mast. The bridge joined the western lands of Arrowwood to the Wilds in the east. The pillars, shaped like elven men with determined grimaces standing in the waters, the bridge hefted on their shoulders and backs, were an amazing sight to behold. Their great eyes appeared to follow the ship as it sailed into the bridge's shadows.

"I don't know why, but those statues give me the chills," Razor said. "Who are they supposed to be? They look tired and angry."

"Those are tributes to the builders. Building a bridge so vast was a mighty task. It spanned decades." Bowbreaker pointed at the faces as the ship passed to the other side of the bridge. "They're also the guardians of the basin, keeping the waters safe for travel. That is Anonulus, the lead builder who became king after the bridge was built. They built the bridge after a long war. Peace followed between the east and west for centuries, at least until Queen Esmarelda came."

Razor lifted his eyes. "Well, those men look tired. Imagine holding a bridge on your back every day. Talk about a boring life."

"They aren't alive." Gorva gave Razor a disappointed snarl. "They're chiseled from stone."

"I know that, but they look real enough to me." Razor leaned back, stretching his spine. "Say, why don't we dock this ship and get something good to eat? I'm tired of corn-meal biscuits. Besides, I hear the elves make wonderful food."

Tatiana shook her head. "We won't be stopping. It's too risky."

Captain Luhey turned over the wheel to one of his crewmen and joined them on the bow. "It's a rare thing for a ship to pass through without stopping at the docks. The Elven Fleet will be tracking every ship that comes and goes. A ship that does not stop on a long journey is suspicious," Captain Luhey offered.

"He's correct," Bowbreaker admitted.

"Aye, the journey is long, and it won't hurt to gather more supplies. The main ports run along Doverun. Smaller ones lie beyond the outskirts of the city. It won't be suspicious if we dock at one of those. A few hours on the land will do us some good," the captain said.

"What do you think?" Tatiana asked Zora.

"I wouldn't mind walking on solid ground again." Zora studied the basin's waters. Seacraft of all sorts spread out among the waters—fishing boats, merchant ships, elven warships, and small sailing boats. She'd never seen so many ships before. She eyed the captain. "So long as it's the routine exercise."

"Oh, it is. I promise you that. Again, several hours on the docks to replenish our stock won't garner any unwanted attention." Captain Luhey tapped the ash off his cigar. He patted his belly. "And I suggest we all have one hot meal." He gave them a hopeful look. "The elves are very accommodating in Doverun."

"I'm fine with it." Zora was more than fine with it. She could use a hot meal in a greasy tavern as much as anyone.

Razor clapped his hands together. "Now we're talking!"

He threw his arm over Captain Luhey's shoulders. "Take me to the tavern with the prettiest elven barmaids."

"That won't be hard. They're all pretty." Captain Luhey waved his arm in the air and caught the attention of his crew. "Man the oars, sailors! We're going in for a taste of Doverun!"

The crew cheered in delight. "Hooray!"

Tatiana nodded at Zora. "A hot meal will do us all some good."

Zora joined Bowbreaker on the port side of the bow. The striking elf had the countenance of a king and the build of a true warrior. Her heart fluttered. "So, will you be joining us, or are you going to stay on the ship?"

"I'll stay back," he said.

She sat down on the bow and looked over the basin. "Perhaps I can bring back something for you to eat. Do you desire any elven dishes?"

He gave her a funny look.

"I mean, foods you like, perhaps that you miss. Everyone has a favorite food."

Bowbreaker set his gaze on the distant city of Doverun that overlooked the shores of the basin. "I'm not one for delicacies. To stay strong, I live off the land," he said in his stern manner.

Zora shrugged. "If you say so." She caught the sun gleaming on the emerald spires of the city. "So, that's Doverun. It's beautiful."

Doverun was a city built around many white towers and majestic green rooftops that shined against the sun. The whitewashed stone buildings stretched along the shoreline. The merchant craft sailed toward the city but on a course north of the main docks. The grand city vanished behind the hills as the merchant ship ducked into a wharf a mile or more upriver from the city.

"I guess I'll be getting ready to go. I won't be long. Try not to miss me." Zora started to walk away.

Bowbreaker grabbed her above the elbow in his warm grip. "Don't be long."

"Oh, I won't be." Her fingers dusted over his strong hand. "I can stay if you wish."

"No." He tipped his head toward the wharf. His jaw tightened. "Look. The elves have shamed themselves."

Many elven soldiers walked the wharf and docks wearing chainmail and crimson tunics with black mountains embroidered on the front.

"Queen Esmarelda is behind this abomination," he continued. "She needs to pay for it."

"Is her throne in Doverun?"

"She has a throne in all six cities. She could be sitting on any one of them, though Doverun is the second-most prominent under Staatus. It wouldn't be a surprise if she dwelled here currently."

There was no mistaking the storm brewing in his eyes.

"You aren't going to do anything impulsive, are you?" Zora asked.

Bowbreaker didn't reply.

The merchant ship docked. The gangplank dropped. Zora departed onto the busy dock with the others. She glanced back at the ship. Bowbreaker was gone.

12

THE COMPANY ATE on an outside porch of a small basin tavern with a full view of the docks. Zora, Razor, Gorva, and Tatiana sat on rickety chairs behind oversized bowls of seafood gumbo. A stack of hot, buttery rolls sat in the middle of the table, and the cute elven barmaid couldn't keep Razor and Gorva's ale tankards full.

"What's the matter, Zora?" Tatiana dabbed her mouth with a napkin. "I thought you were starving for a fine meal, and even I admit this one is satisfying, yet you've only had a few spoonfuls."

"She misses Bowbreaker." Razor hiccupped. "Either that or she doesn't want to get chubby again."

Gorva hit Razor on the head with her spoon. "Mind your manners and drink."

"Is that it? Bowbreaker?" Tatiana asked.

"It's not him. I just lost my appetite." Zora's belly groaned.

Razor laughed. "It sounds like your belly's eating you." He flagged the barmaid with a flip of his fingers. He ogled her shapely build. "More ale if you don't mind, princess."

The cute barkeep offered him a comely smile. "Certainly. Will you be staying long? I can recommend a warm place to stay."

Gorva shoved the waitress away. "No, he won't be staying long."

"Say, what'd you do that for?" Razor asked. "We connected."

"No, you didn't," Gorva said.

The barmaid returned with two more tankards. Gorva's heated stare hurried the younger woman off.

Razor grabbed his tankard with two hands. "You need to mind your own business. I can't help it that women like me. It's who I am." He flashed a devilish smile. "Handsome."

Gorva snorted. "Pffft. You're a handsome man who drinks like a halfling."

"Aw, you called me handsome." Razor reached under the table and squeezed her knee. "I knew you'd come around. Ow!" He jerked his hand away. "She pinched me!"

Zora couldn't find it in herself to laugh, but she

managed to swallow a few more spoonfuls of gumbo. She could see the merchant ship off in the distance. The men on the deck looked little bigger than ants. "I don't see him," she uttered.

Tatiana had her back to the wharf and turned in her chair. "Of course you can't see him. Even I can't see that far. What are you worried about, Zora? I'm sure Bowbreaker concealed himself below deck. After all, they're searching for him."

"You didn't see the look in his eyes when we left. Something wasn't right. It shook me."

"Bowbreaker is a very intense person to fall in love with," Tatiana said.

"What?" Zora almost choked on her stew. "Don't be ridiculous. I admit I'm fond of him, and he's very attractive, but in love? That's not for me."

"Mmm-hmmm," Tatiana said playfully.

"Will you stop it? We have more important matters to worry about."

Around a mouthful of roll, Razor said, "Love is a distraction. That's why I keep my relationships short and simple."

"I'm sure the women are every bit as thankful as you are," Gorva quipped, stone-faced.

"I like this new side of you, Gorva. Very charming, like a crocodile laughing."

Captain Luhey wandered from inside the tavern. A cigar burned where he clenched it in the side of his mouth. He spilled ale on his shirt as he drank from his tankard at the same time as he smoked. “Did you hear the scuttlebutt?”

The company offered him blank looks.

“I know why the Black Guard is thicker than fog in the smaller ports. Apparently, they’re like flies on stink everywhere,” he said.

“Well, what is it?” Razor asked.

“Oh, yes.” The captain exhaled a stream of yellow smoke. “Queen Esmarelda has taken permanent residence in Doverun. Apparently, it is a huge deal. Wherever she goes, an army of Black Guards is with her. I believe a parade will happen sometime today.”

SKREEEEEEEEEEEEEE!

The squall of a dragon flying low over the wharfs forced men to hunker down at their tables. Other patrons sitting on the patio dared a look into the sky. Three dragons flew across the basin in spear-tip formation.

SKREEEEEEEEEEEEEE!

Captain Luhey wiped his paw on his belly. “No matter how hard I try, I can’t get used to that sound.”

“Does Bowbreaker know about the queen?” Zora asked.

“I haven’t told him. I only found out moments ago,” Captain Luhey said.

Zora stood up. “Captain, we need to go.”

"But we aren't ready. My men—"

"Your men can drink themselves blind later." She pushed past his belly and picked her way through the chairs. Once she cleared the tavern's entrance, she took off, racing down the narrow street where buildings nestled side by side. She reached the wharf and slowed to a quick walk. "Dirty acorns."

Black Guards stood scattered along the wharf and docks. They manned the short watchtowers, spyglasses in hand.

Eyes down, Zora navigated through the traffic of workers who moved goods on and off the ships. She approached the merchant ship docked alongside the wharf and hurried up the gangplank. Half the crew had stayed on board to prepare the ship for departure.

"Have you seen Bowbreaker?" she asked one of them.

The lazy-eyed man missing half his teeth shook his head.

Zora took the stairs into the bowels of the ship. She searched high and low, calling out, "Bowbreaker? Bowbreaker?" She ended the search and climbed the stairs topside. She began to sweat as the others from the company made their way up the gangplank. "He's not here," Zora told them. "I didn't see his bow and quiver either."

Tatiana placed her hands on Zora's shoulders. "Sister, you need to settle yourself. I'm certain he's fine."

Panting, Zora said, “You didn’t see the look in his eyes.”

“What do you think will happen?” Tatiana asked.

She locked eyes with Tatiana, desperate. “If he found out the queen is near, I have no doubt he’d try to assassinate her.”

13

ZORA STARTED DOWN THE GANGPLANK. She stopped at the bottom and looked up at her friends. "What is everyone waiting on?"

"We can't go tracking him down on a hunch." Razor carried a small barrel on his shoulder. "Besides, he's a ranger and set in his ways. We couldn't stop him if we wanted to."

"I can't believe what I am hearing." Zora balled her fists. "We can't let him do this."

Tatiana came down the gangplank. "We need to wait him out, but we won't wait forever." She reached for Zora.

Zora backed away. "We aren't going to leave him behind."

"Don't let your passion blind you. Bowbreaker has his

own course. We have ours. He wouldn't have left if he didn't understand that. Come aboard, Zora. We will wait as long as we can," Tatiana said.

Zora almost tripped over a huge coil of rope. "No, no, I'm going after him."

"Don't be silly, woman." Gorva stormed down the gangplank. "You're not using your skull. Don't let your heart rule you."

"Aye, listen to her," Razor agreed.

"No." Zora shook her head. "I'm ashamed of you all!" Zora took off running down the wharf. Tears streamed down her cheeks as she raced through the back stretches of road. She ran a long time before she realized she didn't know where she was going. She didn't know anything about Doverun. She finally stopped inside an abandoned alley, her face wet with tears. She pushed her auburn hair out of her eyes. "What in the Flaming Fence am I doing?"

A small group of elven children playing in the street spotted her. Dressed in warm spring clothing, they stood bare-armed and barefoot. They ran up to her, bouncing on their toes, practically dancing. "The queen is coming! The queen is coming! Aren't you going to the parade?"

Zora caught her breath. "I want to, but I'm new to the city, and I fear I'm lost."

The children gasped, slapping their faces with wide-eyed expressions.

"You can come with us." They grabbed her hands and started towing her along. "Wipe those tears away. The queen is coming."

With a cloak over his shoulders hiding the quiver on his back, Bowbreaker wandered toward Doverun. He'd unstrung his bow, a feat only he could do, and used it like a walking staff. Slouched over, he half dragged his foot behind him, keeping his face hidden underneath his hood.

The call to destiny was at hand. The moment he overheard the dockworkers speaking about the welcome parade for Queen Esmarelda, he knew what he had to do—kill the queen.

Queen Esmarelda was an abomination to elvenkind, a blot against their bright sky. She was a demanding taskmaster with a lust for wealth and power. She'd come into supremacy through assassination and deception. She'd married well—married well and killed. In over five hundred years, none had risen to challenge her. Five hundred years ago, Bowbreaker's bloodline had been killed off by the usurper. Now, the time had come for him to kill her before she killed him first.

The walk to Doverun was long, but he knew the way. He crossed the majestic hills overlooking the shiny waters of the basin and gazed upon the majestic city of Doverun, its streets paved in green stone as far as the eye could see.

He took a twisting road leading into town, and he wasn't alone. Many elves walked on foot, eager to see the queen. Their comments left a taste in his mouth as foul as swamp water.

"They say her beauty is without rival!"

"Her hair is spun from gold."

"She's our king's savior."

"Without a doubt, the greatest ruler of all time."

"Black Frost and Queen Esmarelda forever!"

It took all Bowbreaker had to resist busting their teeth with his bow. His pointed ears burned like fire. *How can my kind be such fools?*

The base of the hills met the streets, and a swell of people hurried toward the center of town.

Bowbreaker couldn't remember the last time he'd seen so many elves in one place. It wasn't without consequences. With their children on their shoulders, parents bumped and trampled over one another. Fights broke out among them. Shame filled him.

Black Guards moved among the people on foot and horseback. They jammed their spear butts into chests in the unruly crowd. The real troublemakers were trampled and dragged away to the rousing cheers of the mob.

One of the Black Guard horsemen spotted Bowbreaker

and led his horse toward the elf. He flagged down another rider on the opposite side of Bowbreaker.

They closed in, shouting, "You there, with the staff, halt! I say halt!"

14

BOWBREAKER LOWERED his bow and sank below the crowd's shoulders. He moved through the press, angling away from the Black Guard. He spotted a gap between the buildings, slowly crept into the narrow seam, and hunkered down behind a water barrel.

The pair of Black Guard riders rode in front of the gap. They turned their heads, searching the throng of people.

"Where'd he go?" one of the soldiers asked.

"I have no idea. What did you see?" asked the other rider.

"He was a big elf with a large walking stick, and he had his face hidden. I wanted a closer look," the elven soldier said. "You need to learn to pay attention to these things. He was nearest you."

The second elven rider turned his horse and faced the

alley. "Hah. You're blaming me for losing an old man and his cane. Is there no one you won't harass?"

"That's my duty. Besides, we're supposed to investigate anything suspicious." The first soldier joined the other in front of the alley. "Watch my horse. I need to relieve myself." He dismounted and wandered into the alley. He stopped in front of the barrel and leaned his arm against the wall. "I've been doing this a long time. If something stands out, you need to check it. It might be nothing, but it's better to be safe than sorry. You never know when it might come to bite you later."

Covered in his cloak, Bowbreaker made himself as small as he could on the other side of the barrel. He could hear the elf pee.

"Sure, sure," the second rider said. "As soon as you finish, I'll be sure to inspect every crone with a cane."

The first rider adjusted his trousers. "Make light of it if you wish, but you'd be wise to listen to a veteran like me. You saw the man the same as I, and he vanished. We called out to him, but he disappeared. Explain that."

"I see your point. Perhaps this old man was a wizard, come to assassinate the queen."

"Don't ever let someone hear you say that." The first rider wandered back out of the alley. "Such talk is considered treason."

"Surely you can't be serious."

"I've seen Black Guards punished for less. We live in

dangerous times. At least we're on the winning side of the fight." The first rider mounted his horse. "And don't call me Surely. It's Anvis."

"Funny, Anvis." The second rider chuckled. "Glad you found your sense of humor. Now let's go hunt down that troublesome stick-wielding beggar."

"You don't want to be a soldier, do you?"

"I want to be a troubadour. Women love troubadours. I wrote some new songs. Would you like to hear them?"

"Luke the Lute Player"—Anvis shook his head—"now I've heard it all."

The Black Guard riders moved on.

Bowbreaker slunk deeper into the alley. He tossed his bow to the top of the roof and scaled the stone walls like a squirrel. His strong fingers found purchase between the rocks and mortar. He made it to the top in no time.

The skies looked empty, but he'd heard the dragon call earlier. He didn't need to get close to the queen's parade. He only needed to get high and have a full view of the street. He slowly looked left and right and spotted a bell tower near the center of the city.

Using the rooftops like a roadway, he made his way toward the bell tower, taking giant leaps from building to building and landing on cat feet. He checked the skies constantly and moved cautiously, picking his moment when the way looked clear. Sudden movement caught prying eyes, and he was well aware that Black Guard soldiers could be posted anywhere, keeping an eye on the streets.

The lone bell tower in Doverun overlooked the main street that ran the length of the city. It stood near one hundred feet high, and the only entrance was through a door at the bottom. The Black Guard had it surrounded.

Bowbreaker would have to find another way in or take his shot at the queen from somewhere else.

With the help of the elven children, Zora went straight into the heart of the crowded city. She had a lot on her mind, but even so, she soaked up the intricate details of the marvelous place. Every building was a work of beauty with its unique flair. Colorful flags and banners waved on the tops of buildings and hung over the storefronts. Flower boxes decorated windows, and the wooden shutters bore bright and vibrant colors. The streets paved with smooth stones had not so much as a single pothole.

BONG!

"Come on, hurry! The parade is starting!" the elated children cried.

BONG!

The bell tower continued to chime.

Hand in hand, the children snaked through the masses, dragging Zora along like she was one of their own. To her amazement, they made it to the edge of a broad street that was empty aside from Black Guard horsemen and foot soldiers pushing people back out of the way.

At the far end, to the south, the parade began with a marching band and lavishly dressed women spinning flaming batons and doing acrobatics.

Zora tried to peel her hands from the children's sticky fingers. She pulled away only to have them grab her fingers an instant later.

Bouncing up and down, they said, "Watch the parade! Watch the parade!"

"I'm watching!" she responded. Tens of thousands of people stretched for as far as the eye could see. Bowbreaker could be hiding anywhere, but it would be impossible to get a shot from the ground. Too many soldiers would see him, and no doubt the queen would be under heavy guard.

An elven girl climbed up on her shoulders. "What are you doing?"

"Getting a better view," the little girl said in a peppy voice.

Zora kept peeling children's fingers away from her own. "I'm never having children."

"What?" the little girl asked.

"Nothing." She needed to find Bowbreaker. It was an impossible task, but he had to be watching the same parade she was. *If I were an assassin, where would I be?*

15

BONG!

Zora whipped around and spotted the bell tower looming in the distance. It had a perfect view of the parade road, but it was too far away to house any sort of threat.

SKREEEEEEEEEE!

A grand dragon dove from the sky and buzzed down the street over the heads of the ducking crowd. The Risker in the saddle pumped his fist in the air as the dragon lifted back up into the sky.

The muted crowd gathered their courage and started cheering again. The girl locked onto Zora's shoulders and shouted, "That was fantastic! I want to ride a dragon!"

"You'll have to settle for a part-elf instead." She started walking away from the parade.

"Where are we going? We'll miss the parade!" the child said.

"I need to find a friend of mine."

The elven girl's upside-down face appeared in front of Zora. "I can help you. I'm a good lookout. I always win when we play hide and chase. I'm the best. What does this friend look like?"

"He's a boy, older like me, really big." Zora forced her way through the people. "Look on the roofs and into the windows."

The girl lifted her hand over her eyes. "I don't think I'm going to be able to find him without a little more detail. Does he have tattoos, or is he missing teeth? What color is his hair? Does he part it on the side or in the middle? What sort of clothing does he wear? Does his body have any distinguishing marks? Perhaps is he missing a limb? Or is he missing an eye? That would be easy to find. Not many people are missing an eye."

"He has coal-black hair, would be carrying a long stick, like a bow, and most likely is wearing a cloak."

"A cloak on a warm day like this?" The girl shrugged. "That makes it easier." She started gently drumming on Zora's head. "No, no, no, no, no..."

Zora smiled. The innocent child had somehow brightened her day. "What's your name?"

"Abigale," the child said brightly. She leaned down. "What's yours?"

"Zora."

"Ooh, Zora. I like that." Abigale started toying with Zora's ears. "You aren't all elf, are you?"

"No, only part."

"What happened to the other part?"

Zora shrugged. "I don't know. I never thought about it." Driven by gut instinct, she continued toward the bell tower. "I'm an orphan."

"Me too!"

A hole opened in the pit of Zora's stomach. She remembered how hard life was on the street when she'd been abandoned. She grabbed Abigale's ankle and squeezed it. "Bless you, child."

The bell tower stood two adjacent blocks away from the main road, where the crowds no longer swelled, but it overlooked all the buildings. Zora cut through the streets and stopped at a shop catty-corner to the bell tower. Several Black Guards were posted in front of the tower's entrance. Most were elves, but a lizardman and an orc stood among them.

"Bowbreaker's not going to get a shot from inside there," she uttered. "Either they're ensuring that, or they're protecting something else." She spied the top of the tower and squinted. Soldiers nested in the tower. "Anvils. Dead end."

Abigale tugged on Zora's ear. "Pardon me, but is that your friend?"

Zora followed the path of the child's small pointing finger. Her heart skipped. Bowbreaker crouched on a rooftop overlooking the bell tower's entrance. Concealed in the bell tower's shadow, he appeared to be stringing his bow.

"What in the world is he going to do?" She took a knee and said to Abigale, "This is where you get off, little friend." She pressed some coins into the girl's hands. "Go enjoy the parade."

Abigale looked at the coins and grinned from ear to ear. "Thank you! Thank you! Thank you! I'm rich!" She ran away, vanishing around the corner.

Zora turned her gaze toward Bowbreaker. Once again, he was gone. "How does he do that?"

Bowbreaker dropped down from the rooftops into the empty streets. He took a knee and undid the cloth he'd used to disguise his bow. Once he unspooled the bowstring from his leather pouch, he hooked the loop in the bottom notch of the ashwood. He ran two fingers along the wood's dark grain. The bow had been in his family for centuries. The wood was cut from the great trees deep in the heart of the Willowwacks. It was as hard as steel and had scarring all over from decades of service.

With a grunt, he braced the bow between his bearskin

boots and bent it. The taut muscles in his oversized right arm flexed. Veins bulged in the round bicep of his tanned skin. The stiff wood started to give. Bowbreaker was the only mortal man alive who could bend the shaft.

As smooth as silk, he slipped the string over the top notch. The bow was ready. He plucked the string. It made a tight twang. He touched the bow to his head and closed his eyes.

Bowbreaker's time had come. His destiny would be fulfilled—or he would die.

He opened the flap of his leather pouch and found a jar little bigger than his thumb. He removed the cork, revealing an inky-black paste. He dipped two fingers into the paste and painted stripes under his eyes on his cheeks and face. The substance caused a burning sensation that penetrated the skin and set his blood on fire. He shed his cloak and smeared the paste onto his arms and chest. He put the jar away and rubbed his fingers dry.

SKREEEEEEEEEE!

SKREEEEEEEEEE!

SKREEEEEEEEEE!

A trio of grand dragons soared low over the buildings. They buzzed by the bell tower and headed back over the ongoing parade.

There was no mistaking their intentions. They were scouring the rooftops for trouble. It would be difficult to avoid them.

Bowbreaker inspected his quiver full of arrows. The shafts' feathers were dipped in black. The tips were made from the same metal as the armor the Sky Riders wore and kissed with magic and dragon's breath. He slung his quiver over his back, notched an arrow, and stepped out into the street.

16

Zora crept up behind Bowbreaker, hooked his elbow, and pulled him out of the street. "Surprise!" she whispered.

Bowbreaker spun around, clamped his hand under her chin, and shoved her into the wall. His eyes burned like wildfire. "What are you doing?" he said in a throaty voice.

"Stopping you from killing yourself."

"That won't happen." He let her go and peeked around the corner at the bell tower. "I can handle them."

"You'll be spotted, and it will be over for all of us. What is on your face?"

"It's called Ranger's Blood. It heightens my senses." His nostrils flared. "Time is short. I must act."

"Give me a moment. If you want to get into that tower, you'll need a distraction." She instinctively touched her neck. The Scarf of Shadows was gone. She'd given it to Grey Cloak. "Acorns."

"What do you have in mind, Zora? My destiny is at hand. I must act quickly, or the opportunity will pass."

She opened Crane's satchel and rummaged through it, finding a ring of keys, the locator medallion box, candles, a small steel spyglass, small balls with an eggshell coating, and a few other trinkets. She held one of the balls in her hand. "I think I know what these do."

Bowbreaker's grimace deepened. "I don't have time for this. My blood burns."

Zora had never seen him lathered up before. His chest heaved, his neck veins bulged, and the muscles in his arms looked like they were going to burst from his skin. She tried to keep a level head, but her heart raced. "Listen to me. We need to wait until the dragon cries again. We can't let the eyes in the tower see this."

"I won't wait another—"

SKREEEEEEEE!

"And you won't have to!" Zora jetted into the street and flung the balls at the Black Guards' feet. The round devices exploded in a cloud of blue dust and a bright flash.

Bamf!

The stunned guards stumbled, coughed, and stammered. Many fell to their knees.

Bowbreaker and Zora hurried to the bell tower into the cover of the rising cloud. The bell tower door was locked.

She took out the ring of keys, picked one, stuffed it in the lock, and twisted. "Not that one."

"Hurry," Bowbreaker urged.

"What does it look like I'm doing? This is a big lock. I think I need a bigger key." She found a key that matched the hole. "This should do it." She stuffed it in the keyhole and twisted. The latch popped. "After—*ulp*."

Bowbreaker shoved the door open, pulled her inside, and locked the door. Without a word, he ran like a deer up the staircase that spiraled up the inner circle of the wall.

Zora peeked through the keyhole at the stunned Black Guards. She'd seen Tanlin use the Balls of Thunder before on another mission. Not only did they stun people, but they caused brief memory loss as well. The soldiers outside shook their heads and rubbed their eyes. They didn't appear to suspect a thing as they shared some uneasy looks with one another and resumed their posts. "Perfect." She took off after Bowbreaker.

Halfway up the stairs, her legs started to burn. She huffed for breath and slowed to a walk. Her lungs were on fire. "Anvils." She gasped as she peeked up the spiral stairway. "How'd he get up there so fast?" Something dropped from the top of the tower.

A Black Guard plummeted toward the tower floor and crashed into the hard ground.

"Whoa." Zora leaned over the stair's edge. Another body sailed right by her head. She jumped back and yelled upward. "Do you mind? A little warning would help!" A rush of blood washed away her fatigue. She stormed up the steps. "When I get to the top, he's going to get a talking-to."

By the time Zora reached the top, she was so winded she could barely climb through the doorway. Her knees quaked as she crawled across the floor. "Thanks for waiting," she gasped.

A third Black Guard lay dead on the wooden floor with his neck broken. He was orcen.

Zora had to crawl over him to join Bowbreaker. "Ew. He stinks. Couldn't you have tossed him down too?"

The brass tower bell stood taller than a man and hung over the gap. Ropes to ring it were tethered to the wall. Coils of rope that could be tossed down to ring the bell from below lay piled on the floor. Bowbreaker stood in the tower's window, bow in hand, watching the parade.

Zora joined him. She could see the entire city and had a perfect view of the festive parade from a southern angle. "Nice view. Everyone looks so small from here."

Bowbreaker notched an arrow, his face a mask of concentration.

"What are you aiming at?" she asked.

The people were so tiny it was impossible to distinguish one from another. She removed the spyglass from the satchel and extended the lens. She could make out faces and even spotted the children she'd been with. "Whoa, this is much better."

Zora stood to the right of Bowbreaker. Cords of muscle popped out in his forearm as he pulled the bowstring back along his cheek.

"Are you sure this is the only way? It's murder."

"No," he said in a voice as cold as ice, "it's vengeance."

17

A ROUSING explosion of cheers came up from the people in the streets. It started at the beginning of the parade at the top end of the city as the people's voices filled the air with hungry glee. The queen was coming.

Using the spyglass, Zora watched the fantastic parade. Corps of drummers marched down the street, followed by horn and flute players. Dancers ran and jumped, using sticks with colorful ribbons at the top. The costumes and uniforms were spectacular, showy, and outrageous. The music echoed off the buildings like beautiful thunder, and everyone smiled, perhaps too much.

A sliver of doubt crept into her as she watched the joyful faces scream and shout. Doverun was beautiful. *How wrong could it be?* "Is this the right thing?" she muttered.

Bowbreaker relaxed the bowstring. "You will see the truth. The truth will set them free," he replied.

Zora swallowed the knot in her throat. Her skin pricked all over as she watched the trio of dragons circle the sky above. She followed the parade from the front to the end. Her gaze rested on the queen's lavish golden float surrounded by soldiers in golden platemail armor marching along the float, carrying spears high. Queen Esmarelda sat on a pure ivory throne, modestly waving at the crowd with a subtle side-to-side twist of her hand.

A golden crown studded with jewels and diamonds rested on the queen's honey-kissed hair. The older elven woman's porcelain skin was without blot or blemish. Her refined features were graceful and gorgeous. With a captivating smile, her red lips blew kisses to the crowd. She wore an elegant sun-gold gown beaded with silver raindrops.

"She's breathtaking," Zora muttered.

"She's evil," Bowbreaker replied.

The procession continued down the main street with the adoring crowd wildly waving at Queen Esmarelda. A male elf rushed into the street, running at the queen's float with a bouquet of flowers. The Golden Sentries pounced, beat the man down, and dragged his limp body from the street. The float rolled over the broken man's flowers and proceeded slowly down the street. It passed the halfway point when Zora heard the bowstring stretch.

Oy, this is really happening.

She dropped the spyglass from her eye. The queen was too far for Bowbreaker to make such a long shot. "What if the arrow fails? It might hit an innocent person in the crowd."

"It won't," he said. With two strong fingers hooked on the string, he pulled back several more inches. His oversized arm flexed. Muscle on muscle swelled beneath his skin. Bowbreaker stood as sturdy as a steel wall and took aim.

Zora put the spyglass over her eye. She looked down at the queen with a trembling hand.

I'm going to witness an assassination firsthand. I can't watch. I can't not watch!

Queen Esmarelda sat in her throne, pure and innocent, oblivious to the call of death coming for her. All of a sudden, her warm gaze turned intense, and her pale eyes glowed. She looked straight into Zora's eye. A chill spread through her limbs.

The bowstring snapped. A black arrow sailed. The shaft impaled Queen Esmarelda through the heart. The arrow buried itself feather-deep in her chest. The queen's head sank, her body pinned to the chair.

Bowbreaker lowered his bow. "It is done."

Many Golden Sentries rushed to the queen's float. The enthralled crowd began to quiet. Someone screamed. More frightened cries followed.

"We need to go," Bowbreaker ordered. He reached for Zora.

She pulled away and replied, "No, wait."

A commotion started on the float. The queen's hands and arms moved. She shoved the Golden Sentries away like they were children. She recaptured Zora's gaze with fire in her eyes.

"Sweet dragons," Zora uttered. "She's alive."

Bowbreaker swung his gaze back toward the parade and notched another arrow. "Now the people will see the true face of their queen."

Queen Esmarelda pointed at the bell tower. She shouted angry words at her soldiers. With her bare hand, she snapped the black feathers from the arrow and pulled her body free from the chair. Her countenance became evil. Her body pulsed and flexed as her porcelain skin split and cracked. Bowbreaker let another arrow fly. It impaled the queen's chest once more, knocking her back into her chair.

"Oh my!" Zora watched a horrific transformation right before her eyes.

A black forked tongue rolled out of the queen's mouth. Horns grew on her head, and black bat wings sprouted through the back of her gown. Her body burst inside her dress, and she grew into a gross, demonic elven form.

The panicked citizens of Doverun ran and screamed.

Twang!

Another arrow sailed true and punched a new hole in the monster queen's chest.

Zora gasped. "What is she?"

"Not mortal flesh and blood, or my arrows would have killed it."

SKREEEEEEEE!

SKREEEEEEEE!

Riskers flew straight for the tower.

"Go!" Bowbreaker demanded. He tossed the rope down. "Hurry!"

"What about you?"

Bowbreaker took aim. "I'll be fine. Those dragons don't know what they're in for."

Zora jumped for the rope, grabbed it, and shimmied down. The great bell rang.

BONG!

The earsplitting sound loosened her grip. She plummeted toward the ground.

18

ZORA'S FINGERS clawed at the rope and fastened. She snagged it with her hands and slid down the fibers. The skin of her palms burned like fire. She came to a stop, groaned, and looked down. She'd dropped almost halfway down the tower before she'd secured herself. Sweat dripped from her chin. She looked up. The bell still rocked.

BONG!

Soundwaves rocked her body, but she tightened her stingy grip. She saw no sign of Bowbreaker. She swung gently back and forth on the rope. "What is he doing up there, waiting for the parade?"

A soldier shouted at her from below, "You there!"

The Black Guards guarding the tower had gathered on the ground floor. Eight men in all, armed with swords and spears.

Zora shouted back, "Yes? Can I help you?"

An elven soldier pointed his sword at her. "Get down here or die!"

With her legs wrapped around the rope like an acrobat, she leaned away with one arm. "I don't think either of those options sounds very accommodating. Is there a third?" she hollered. "Perhaps something more sensible?"

Two soldiers started climbing the stairs.

The elven soldier sneered. A ninth soldier—a brutish orc—entered through the tower's doorway, carrying a crossbow. He handed it to the elf, who quickly loaded it and took aim.

"Introducing option number three," he said.

Zora's eyes grew big. "I guess that's what my smart mouth gets me."

The trio of grand dragons buzzed past the tower, roaring as loud as thunder. The tower bell hummed. The lead dragon broke away, and one of the others came right at Bowbreaker.

Bowbreaker took aim and fired. His arrow whizzed through the sky and punctured deep into the dragon's left eye.

The beast bucked in midair and tossed its Risker from the saddle. The rider plunged toward the street. The enraged dragon roared, twisted in midair, and flew straight for the tower with its horns lowered.

With the Ranger's Blood coursing through his veins, Bowbreaker loaded another arrow and fired the next instant. The arrow hit the dragon's right pupil and sank all the way to the feathers.

The dragon's wings stiffened. Its momentum carried it on a path sailing straight toward Bowbreaker. He jumped twenty feet to the other side of the bell tower's platform. The dragon crashed into the tower, horns first. The structure shook. Walls of stone shifted. The bell rang.

BONG!

Its great jaws pushed deeper into the tower. The blind dragon's nostrils sniffed out Bowbreaker, and it shoved its head in farther, horns hitting the bell, hungry jaws snapping together.

BONG!

Bowbreaker sprinted forward. He grabbed the shaft protruding from the dragon's left eye and pushed it deeper into the monster's skull.

The dragon convulsed and spasmed. Its huge body went limp. Claws scraped over stone, ripping out blocks and mortar, as the dragon slipped away and fell down the side of the tower. It hit the ground hard.

THUD!

Bowbreaker's ears pricked. Risker arrows whistled toward him. He ducked one, but another clipped a hunk of skin from his shoulder. He took cover behind the bell, slipped another arrow from his quiver, and loaded it as smooth as silk. Arrows ricocheted off the tower bell.

Tang! Tang! Tang! Tang!

Bowbreaker stepped out and fired. His arrow found a new home between the platemail armor covering the Risker's ribs. He released another shaft, hitting the same man in the back as the new attacker and his dragon dropped out of sight.

Loading another arrow, Bowbreaker crept toward the ledge and looked down. The dragon and Risker clung to the tower's walls, its serpent eyes looking right at him. Its jaws opened wide.

Bowbreaker fired into its mouth just as a geyser of flames spewed out. He jumped back from the heat. The suffocating fire kept coming as the dragon crammed its head into the tower's opening. The flames spread into the bell tower room, consuming everything they touched, setting the wood floor and ceiling on fire.

BONG!

The elven soldier squeezed the trigger on the crossbow.

Zora jerked to the side. The arrow zipped by her ear. "Zooks, he's a good shot."

Black Guards raced up the stairs in heavy armor. They

didn't make it a quarter of the way up before they had to clutch their sides.

Zora swung on the rope. "Come on, fellas. I'm waiting." Holding the rope with one hand, she rummaged through the satchel with the other.

The elven soldier locked the crossbow string into place. He dropped another bolt into the slot and raised the weapon to his shoulder. "I won't miss a second time."

Zora's fingers found another Thunder Ball. She tossed it down. "Catch."

He squeezed the trigger.

Clatch-zip!

The bolt sailed true. She tried to twist out of the way. It tore into her side. "Guh!"

Bamf!

The Thunder Ball stunned every man standing on the floor. The hollow walls of the tower amplified its concussive force, knocking them off their feet. A blue cloud of smoke rose from the incident and past Zora.

She hung on for dear life and looked down. The bolt had gone in one side of her abdomen and stuck out the other. "That's bad."

ROOOOAAAAAR!

Zora gazed up. The top level of the bell tower was consumed in flames. The rope had caught fire. "That's worse."

Hand after hand, she climbed down, sheer pain

shooting through her abdomen. She saw no sign of Bowbreaker. *Where is he?*

Two Black Guards stood on the stairs below her, waiting with spears.

Don't they ever give up?

The rope jerked as the flames up top consumed it. The timbers that held the bell in the tower popped and groaned. The huge bell wobbled above her.

"Horseshoes! It's going to fall!" She climbed down faster with dozens of feet still between her and the ground. "Anvils! I'm not going to make it."

The Black Guard waiting on the steps sniggered. "Come on, little woman, jump. Don't worry, we'll catch you."

19

DRAGON FLAME ATE the tower's wooden innards and turned planks to ash. Smoke and fire consumed everything. Fighting his way through the raging heat, Bowbreaker climbed into the rafters and pushed open the portal at the top.

The fresh air sucked up more smoke and flame. He scrambled onto the slanted rooftop and slid down the tiles. His bearskin boots found purchase, and his body came to a stop.

A quick glimpse below revealed people clearing the streets, running for shelter. He leaned over the roof's edge. The pursuing dragon's head was still stuck in the tower's opening. It clung to the tower like a great lizard stuffing its head into the knothole of a tree.

SKREEEEEEEE!

The lead dragon circled the tower. The Risker in the saddle spotted Bowbreaker and pointed up at him. He pulled the dragon's reins, and they came his way. The Risker loaded his bow.

With his bow slung over his back, Bowbreaker jumped off the tower. He landed on the arrow-riddled Risker clinging to the tower below in a crash of metal and brawny limbs. He hoped to knock the warrior from his saddle, but the strong elf held on tight.

"Nice try, but you will die, Bowbreaker!" The elven Risker headbutted Bowbreaker with the brim of his open-faced helmet.

Warm blood ran from his nostrils as he battled the Risker, trying to shove him off. The dragon peeled away from the tower and took flight.

The Risker snuck out a dagger and stabbed at Bowbreaker's gut. "Die, outlaw, die!"

"You first, elven traitor!" He seized the warrior's wrist with his strong right hand and turned the dagger around. He saw the whites of the elf's fear-filled eyes.

The Risker fought back, but his strength was no match for Bowbreaker's. "You can't do this! I am a Risker!"

"You live for evil!" Bowbreaker said above the wind. He forced the Risker's dagger into the gut of the elf's platemail armor. "You die for evil!"

The Risker's face paled. His grasp slipped from the reins, and he fell out of the saddle.

Bowbreaker wasted no time. He stood on the dragon's back and notched an arrow. He fired into the back of the dragon's skull one arrow after another.

Thwack! Thwack! Thwack!

The great beast lurched in midair. Its wings remained spread, instinctively flapping as death slowly spread through its body. He braced himself, clinging to the dragon's saddle. It leaned sideways, wings clipping the building tops, and chimneys crashed onto the road leading to the bell tower. Bowbreaker slid down to the ground, feeling nothing but pain from top to bottom.

SKREEEEEEEEEE!

He looked up. The last dragon, the leader, came for him, its Risker standing up in his saddle's stirrups. Bowbreaker ran for the tower.

The lizardman Black Guard standing on the stairs stretched his spear toward Zora. "Grab ahold, and we'll pull you in." His thin tongue flicked out of his mouth. "We won't hurt you. I promise."

At the top of the tower, the rope burned. Dragon fire ate it up fast. Zora could feel vibrations in the rope as the fibers gave way. She climbed down faster.

The soldiers came down the steps as fast as she climbed.

"You're running out of time, pretty thing," the lizardman said.

"She's not going to come. She'd rather fall." The elven soldier poked out his spear. "I say kill her, and let's watch her fall."

"Why not? It's been a long enough day already." The lizardman took a poke.

Zora kicked the spear away. "If I weren't hanging from a rope, I'd kill you both."

The Black Guards laughed. "I like her. She has fire. A shame it won't last."

An arrow lodged itself deep in the lizardman's chest.

Thunk!

The same fate befell the elf.

Thunk!

Both soldiers fell over the side of the stairs.

Zora cast a bewildered look downward and saw Bowbreaker standing at the base of the stairwell. She did a double take, looking up then down. "How did you get down there?"

"I flew." He closed them inside. "Now climb down. Hurry!"

She resumed her descent. The rope snapped.

Zora plunged through the heart of the tower. "Aieeey!"

Bowbreaker caught her in his arms.

"Guh!" she gasped painfully.

He noticed the arrow in her side. "You're wounded."

"Hardly a scratch. Thanks for catching me."

The timbers in the tower top popped and cracked. She glanced up. The tower bell was coming down.

"Bowbreaker, move!"

He jumped out of the bell's path in a single leap. The huge bell hit the floor on its side and chimed one final chime.

BONG!

It rolled in front of the door, trapping them inside.

She slid out of his arms. "I hope you killed all those dragons."

"All save one. We need to treat your wound while we have a moment." He looked her in the eye and grabbed her waist. "This will hurt."

Caught up in his dark gaze, she asked, "What will hurt?"

He yanked the bolt out of her body.

She screamed. "Ow!" She grasped her bloody side. "I could have used a warning."

"No time for that." Using two fingers, he applied the black paste called Ranger's Blood to both sides of her wound. "This will stop the bleeding, and it—"

"Burns! Thanks for the warning." Her chest heaved, and she caught her breath. Her body felt like it was on fire from head to toe. Her hands were skinned raw, and she wanted to vomit. She broke out in a cold sweat and grabbed Bowbreaker's arm to steady herself. "This is your fault."

"You would be safe now if you hadn't come after me." He studied their surroundings. "Why did you?"

"If you don't know, you're a fool." She walked away from him and looked at the bell blocking the door. "I don't suppose you can use that big arm of yours to move this."

"There's a dragon and Risker on the other side. No telling what else." He put his salve in his pouch.

She leaned against the bell and crossed her arms. "I guess this is it. We're trapped."

More burning cinders fell from above and crashed off the bell to the floor.

Zora sighed. *Of all the men to fall for, I pick one with a head like stone.*

"Bowbreaker!" a raw voice called from above. The demonic form of Queen Esmarelda stood at the top of the steps with her arms and bat-like wings spread. "Your time to die has come!"

20

ZORA HAD NEVER SEEN a creature so horrifying. The radiant elven woman she'd seen in the parade had been fully replaced by a black-winged demon bursting with raw muscle. Its hands had turned into talons eager to rip flesh apart. Brown bumpy spots covered its thick skin.

Bowbreaker took aim.

"If those arrows didn't hurt her the first time, what makes you think they will this time?" Zora asked.

"We don't have much choice, do we?" he asked.

WHAM!

Something rocked the tower door from the outside. It shook the frame of the entire building.

"What was that?" she asked.

"I believe the dragon is trying to get in."

"This must be a popular place."

WHAM!

The tower trembled.

Bowbreaker fired. His arrow sank into the demon's chest. He fired one arrow after another.

The queen continued her downward trek and landed on the ground. "Your arrows can't harm me!" she gloated with open arms. "I'm invincible!"

He lowered his bow. "You aren't the queen. What are you?"

"I'm a guardian changeling from the Nether Realm, summoned by wizards," the evil creature said in a haunted, echoing voice.

Bowbreaker nodded. "That's all I needed to know."

He snaked an arrow from his quiver. Its head was shaped like a crescent moon. Runes of green energy came alive around the tip. He loaded it onto his string and fired. The streak of bright green hit the guardian in the chest, swamping it in radiant green fire.

"Noooo!" it screamed. "Noooooooo!" Its body expanded and convulsed. It stormed forward, its limbs turning to stone, and crumbled into pieces.

"It's dead?" Zora asked.

"Aye."

"What sort of arrow did you shoot it with?"

"Anya and I made preparations back in Safe Haven. I tried to anticipate what I might be facing when I killed the queen." Some of his black-feathered arrows had broken free of the guardian's body. He placed three of them back in his quiver.

"Do you have any more tricks up your sleeve?" Zora asked.

"I don't have sleeves."

WHAM!

The entire tower shook. The walls started to cave in. Stones from the top tumbled down. The walls of the tower buckled and bowed.

WHAM!

"This tower is going to come down!" she said. "We need to get out of here."

Bowbreaker stood with his head up and arms extended at his sides. "I have failed my mission. The Ranger Blood no longer burns," he said boldly as he closed his eyes. "My fate is doom."

"Stop talking like a fool!"

A huge chunk of wall fell a foot from Bowbreaker. Dragon horns burst through the tower wall. The ranger didn't budge. He stood like a statue waiting for the end.

"You've caused enough trouble. I won't have any more of it!"

The tower fell from top to bottom.

Zora swept Bowbreaker off his feet and carried him like a giant child in her arms. She grunted and groaned with every step, carrying him to the mouth of the bell. "Acorns, you're heavy!" She stuffed him inside the bell and crammed herself next to him. She covered her ears, though it still sounded like the world had fallen on top of them.

Stone banged on metal. Their brass shelter shook. Blackness fell upon them. The sound of life muted. They breathed heavily, their two hearts beating as one. Underneath tons of rock, they lived, but they had no clue how long that could last.

Bowbreaker wrapped Zora in his warm arms. "Thank you."

"You're welcome." She nuzzled his chest. "Is this comfortable?"

Bowbreaker began to snore.

"Great. We find some time alone together and now this." She fumbled through Crane's satchel and removed a candle. She blew on the wick. It flamed to life. "Isn't that nice?"

Zora had a full view of Bowbreaker inside their metal grave. The black streaks on his face and arms were smeared. His jaw sagged, and he appeared exhausted. "That Ranger's Blood must have taken a lot out of you." She brushed the hair from his eyes and wiped the smudges from his face. "If I'm going to die in this grave, I hope we get to talk one more time." She pulled her knees to her chest. "Even though you don't talk very much." She yawned.

The hours filled with silence. Finally, she lay down on Bowbreaker, blew out the candle, and fell asleep. It didn't feel longer than a moment had passed before she woke.

Stone scraped on stone. A crack of light shone in. Zora rose and wiped the drool from her mouth. Someone outside was digging. The rubble that buried them inside the bell started to move.

Bowbreaker stirred. He sat up and rubbed his eyes.

Black Guard soldiers carried the rubble away. The soldiers grabbed Zora first and hauled her out.

"Goy! Let go of me!"

A soldier punched her in the gut.

"Oof!" She doubled over and fell to her knees. An army of Black Guards surrounded them. The dragon that had rammed the tower lay still underneath the rubble. More soldiers grabbed Bowbreaker and brought the weakened ranger out.

Someone clapped. "Well done. That was quite a show."

Zora lifted her eyes and found herself gazing at the dazzling Queen Esmarelda dressed in an exquisite all-black gown trimmed with crushed red rubies. Gorgeous rings adorned her elegant fingers. The flawless woman continued, "Bring me Bowbreaker. I want his head."

21

THE FALLEN bell tower had crushed two blocks of buildings. Rubble, dust, and debris had scattered everywhere, and the air was still cloudy. Citizens coughed and cried as they tried to free their kin from the rubble.

Soldiers forced Zora to her knees and tied her hands behind her back. Bowbreaker was put in the same position. They were surrounded by a ring of the queen's Golden Sentries, and Black Guards stood as far as the eye could see. The heroic pair weren't going anywhere.

Queen Esmarelda approached Bowbreaker but stayed well out of harm's way. Her soldiers kept their spears at the ranger's throat. Her beautiful eyebrows knitted together. A snarl marred her perfect face. "We're going to stretch your neck so long you'll look like a dead dragon by the end of the day. You killed my personal guardian, ruined my parade, and wrecked part of my city. We will show you no mercy, my betrothed."

Zora gasped. "Betrothed?"

A Golden Sentry backhanded her.

"Leave her alone!" Bowbreaker said.

A butt from a spear doubled him over.

"Ah." The queen approached and stood in front of Zora. "I have competition." She grabbed Zora's hair and pulled her head back. "An ugly part-elf, of all things. You'd choose this over me?" She released Zora. "Disappointing."

Zora glared at Bowbreaker. "You never told me you had a fiancée."

"I don't. Never trust the word of a witch." Bowbreaker spit. "Especially this one's lying tongue."

Queen Esmarelda swept her honey-blond hair over her shoulder and laughed delightedly. "Who's lying now? Our marriage was arranged since the day we were born, but for some maniacal reason, he resists."

"I can't imagine why," Zora said sarcastically.

A Golden Sentry drew his hand back.

"No," the queen said. "Leave her be. I want her in fair condition when Bowbreaker watches her die. I want his heart to break just as he broke mine."

"You have no heart," he replied.

Zora grinned. *Now he reveals a sense of humor.*

A Black Guard commander approached the queen. He took a knee. "My queen. The others are in custody."

The queen's eyes brightened. "Excellent. Bring them here. I want to meet these assassins face-to-face."

Black Guards brought over Tatiana, Razor, and Gorva and knocked them to their knees.

"Whoa, talk about a queen," Razor said.

"Silence!" A Black Guard commander punched Razor in the jaw.

Razor spit out a tooth. "After all of this, now I lose a tooth." He smiled at the queen. "I don't mind if you don't."

Zora looked down the row at her companions. "Careful, she's engaged to Bowbreaker."

"What is it with women and him? Can't they pick a man less wooden?" Razor remarked.

Queen Esmarelda spoke. "Don't worry, human. We won't be going through with the wedding."

"Well, if you need someone to stand in his place, I'd be happy to—*oof*!"

The commander whacked him again. He jerked Razor up by the hair and put a dagger against his throat. "My queen, let me silence this one permanently."

"Stay your hand," she calmly said. "I'll make an example of them for all to see when they swing from the gallows. It's a shame for you, Bowbreaker. We could have ruled Arrowwood together, but you chose the wrong side. Yet I will live to see tomorrow, and you won't. Did you really think you could slay me? Hah. My eyes for you are everywhere." With a nod, she summoned the part-orc Captain Luhey and elven Captain Cravvit.

Luhey looked guilty with his chin down, but Captain Cravvit's eyes gleamed with triumph.

"Your enemies were right under your nose, and you didn't even know. My trap was set before you even pulled into the wharf. You bit on the parade, hook, line, and sinker. I've tried to win you over, time and again. Many elves think you're their folk hero. But now, you've given me the ammunition I need by attacking me and endangering everyone in the city. All for what, to fulfill a ludicrous destiny? Black Frost laughs at your prophecy, as do I."

"As long as I breathe, there's a chance you won't," Bowbreaker said.

"I don't think so." Queen Esmarelda turned away. "I want them taken straight to the gallows. Their deaths will be my parade's grand finale."

"Well played, Bowbreaker," Razor said as the soldier lifted the company to their feet. "Not only did you fulfill your destiny, but you fulfilled ours as well."

Zora watched the large prisoner wagon pull into view. It was covered in steel bars with two Black Guard soldiers sitting in the front. The passenger jumped out and opened the back of the steel cage.

"Now isn't the time to argue," Zora said.

"I'm not going down without getting a few more licks in

on Stone Face." Razor shuffled along in his shackles. "Or you, for the matter."

"This isn't his fault. We all fell into the trap. We were doomed whether Bowbreaker departed or not," she said.

"No surprise you're making excuses for him."

Two soldiers picked up Razor and tossed him headfirst into the wagon.

"Thanks, fellas. I hope you enjoy the show," he grumbled. "I always wanted to die with steel in hand. Instead, I get a rope around my neck."

Gorva entered the wagon with her hands bound in front of her. "Stop whining. If you must die, die with honor."

"How about I die with one last kiss?" Razor puckered up.

"I'd rather die than see that happen," Gorva replied.

"No need to be so frosty. We're both about to die, you know."

"Not soon enough, apparently."

Razor laughed. "Ah-hahahaha!"

22

A Black Guard locked all five members of Talon inside the prisoner wagon. The strapping woman soldier wore the standard open-faced helm with a row of hard ridges on the top. Her eyes were serious and probing. She tugged on the padlock a few times and hung the key ring from her belt.

"You there." The female Black Guard indicated one of her fellow soldiers. "Gather their gear. We have orders to sink it all in the basin."

A short, stocky man in Black Guard armor rolled up the bow and quiver and Talon's other belongings inside a blanket. He had a big, round face and spoke in an abrasive voice. "Right away, Sergeant." He moved like a little gorilla, picking up the blanket roll and practically waddling over to his woman superior. "Where do you want it?"

"Throw it underneath the bench in the front." The

woman's steady gaze passed over Zora. She shrugged her brows.

Zora sat up. As dire and depressing as their situation was, something about the woman caught her attention. The Black Guard moved with eager purpose and avoided eye contact with the others. With Razor and Gorva bickering in the background, Zora nudged Bowbreaker. His dark gaze slid over to the Black Guards.

"You there!" an aloof Golden Sentry commander said. The lean elf stood tall in his pristine armor and glowered at the able-bodied woman. He approached the prisoner wagon. "Why are you taking their gear?"

The Black Guard soldier snapped her heels together and saluted. "I'm following my commander's orders, Commander."

"Those items are valuable. I'm certain the queen wants the bow and quiver as a prize," the sentry said.

"I will take them straight to the gallows." She gave another quick salute.

Zora noticed the loose fit of the woman's uniform, and the helmet she wore continued to slide on her head. The gorilla-like man that worked with her looked like his beefy build had been stuffed into his chainmail armor and tunic. His sausage fingers kept tugging at his collar. And Zora couldn't shake a familiarity that resonated with the woman, something about her eyes.

"I'll take the bow and quiver directly to the queen. Fetch them for me," the sentry commanded.

"Er… as you wish. Right away, Commander."

The beefy Black Guard stepped up on the back of the wagon and clung to the bars.

The sentry commander looked at him.

The guard tugged on the bars. "I need to test a few rusty spots."

"This wagon doesn't look like a standard prisoner wagon." The commander traced his finger along the outside of the wood. "Where's the inventory stamp?"

"We lost a wheel and took our wagon to the armory." The woman climbed into the bench seat. "This one is a loan."

Clinging oddly to the bars, the male Black Guard nodded agreement. The Black Guard in the driver's seat slouched over and stilled.

"Where is that bow and quiver?" the sentry demanded. "I won't keep the queen waiting."

"One more moment!" she answered. Under her breath, she said to the driver, "Move it. Move it now."

Another prisoner wagon pulled into the area. It was in far better condition and pulled by a team of two brown horses with a pair of Black Guards in the bench seat.

The sentry commander did a double take. "Wait a moment! Who are you? Where did this wagon come from?"

The Black Guard hanging to the bars on the back of the

wagon screamed like a banshee. “Gooooo! What are you milk saps waiting for? A bell to ring! Goooooo!”

The prisoner wagon jumped. Everyone inside slid backward.

“Halt!” the elven sentry said. “Halt!”

The wagon picked up speed. Hooves thundered over the paved streets, and the gray horse pulling the prisoners let out a loud, frightened whinny.

The hairs on Zora’s arms stood on end. She moved to the front and reached through the bars. “Who are you?” She clutched at the driver and looked at the woman.

The Black Guard woman took off her helmet. Long brown hair spilled out. “I’m Shannon, but you used to call me Beak.” She smiled. “My nose healed much better the last time.”

“Yes! I know you from Monarch City! So, who’s this?” Zora’s fingers caught the driver’s helmet, and she flipped it off, revealing a lustrous mound of wavy brown hair. She saw his friendly face. “Crane!”

“Hello, Zora!” He gave a jovial smile. “Did you miss me?”

“I thought you were dead!”

“Would a dead man have gorgeous hair as thick as this?” He gave her a black look. “It’s a long story.”

“But how’d you find us?”

Crane shrugged. “You know me. I have a knack for being in the right place at the right time.”

"Sorry to break up the reunion!" the Black Guard latched onto the back of the wagon said. His helmet flew off, revealing his wiry, wooly hair. "But would it kill you to speed matters along?"

"Who's that?" Zora asked.

"Don't you remember Sergeant Tinison?" Beak answered. "Don't worry. He's loud, but he's a friend."

The Golden Sentries and Black Guards pursued on horseback and foot, the riders gaining.

"I'm about to get my buttocks lanced!" Sergeant Tinison beat on the bars. "Faster!" An arrow struck his rear end. He screamed bloody murder. "Auuuuugh!"

23

"CRANE, if you don't get this wagon rolling faster, I'm going to be a human meat shield!" Sergeant Tinison yelled.

Zora didn't see the black horse pulling the wagon but rather a dapple-gray beast. "What happened to Vixen?"

"Poor Vixen didn't survive the battle with Hella and Steelhammer. Don't worry. Charro is the best there is," he said.

In an alarmed voice, she asked, "Is she a nightmare?"

"No, I bought her in Valley Shire. Isn't she gorgeous?" Crane snapped the reins. "Yah! Charro! Yah!"

Charro surged forward. She turned onto the next block. The wagon skidded over the street and slammed into a fruit stand.

"Are you telling me you can't do your thing?" Zora asked.

"What thing?"

"With the horse whip and the flames?"

"Oh that. I don't think we'll need it."

The enemy riders closed in. They split into different groups and raced down the adjacent streets.

"They're trying to cut us off," Tatiana said. "Shannon, we need our gear."

"Way ahead of you!" Shannon fed Bowbreaker's bow and arrows back through the bars. She gave Zora Crane's satchel.

"Say, I've been looking for that," Crane said.

"You gave it to me, remember?" Zora slung it over her shoulder. "Do you want it back?"

"Of course not. A gift is a gift."

The prisoner wagon raced down street after street. They watched their enemies racing by them on adjacent roads as they passed through intersections.

From a knee, Bowbreaker fired his arrows through the bars. He picked off a horse, downing it, causing a collision among the trailing riders.

"If I had a bow, I'd use it too." Razor buckled on his sword belt. A Golden Sentry on horseback sped along the right side of the wagon. He poked through the bars with his spear.

Gorva yanked the spear away, jerking the man out of his saddle. "Thank you!"

"Thanks, beautiful," Razor said.

"Don't mention it," Gorva replied.

Crane drove the wagon north toward the hills overlooking the Great Basin. The road wound slowly from top to bottom.

"We aren't going to make it up that hill before they catch us!" Zora cried out.

The soldiers that had raced ahead were forming a blockade. Their numbers thickened, hemming in Talon.

Charro labored up the slope in the road.

"The wagon is too heavy." Crane gave Zora the sincerest look. "Sorry, we'll have to take a shortcut. Hold on!" He pulled the reins hard.

Charro turned hard to the left. The wagon skipped over the stones. Charro's hooves raked over the street then found traction. She sped forward into the next street.

Sergeant Tinison locked his arms around the bars, praying with his eyes closed, "Please don't let go. Please don't let go."

The sudden move threw off their pursuers who'd gathered at the end of the next road.

"Crane, it's good to see you, but this is the worst escape plan ever," Zora said.

He shrugged. "I've done worse, if you can imagine."

"I'd rather not." Even if they were to escape, they had nowhere to escape to. They had no ship to sail out of the basin, and the roads would go on for leagues. The armies of Doverun would catch them for certain.

Charro charged up a narrow country road surrounded by steep banks. The wagon rocked and pitched side to side over the bumpy lane. It gave them cover, but Queen Esmarelda's forces closed the gap.

Tatiana produced the Star of Light. The large pink gemstone burned with white fire.

"What will you do with that?" Zora asked.

"The only thing I can do. Summon Anya," Tatiana said.

"If you do that, they'll be exposed."

"I don't think we have a choice."

"Put that thing away!" Crane's eyes sparkled with inner flames. He produced his horse whip and gave it a snap.

Pop!

The horse whip flamed on. Crane grinned.

"I thought you said you couldn't use that anymore," Zora said, exasperated.

"This ride wouldn't be as exciting if it didn't have a few surprises."

Zora couldn't hide her astonishment. She stretched her arms through the bars and choked him. "You've been holding out the entire time? Are you mad?"

"I like to let the enemy think they're winning, then wham! I turn it on!" With his torchlight glimmering in his eyes, he stood up and popped the horse whip across Charro's back. "Hold on, everyone! It's time to ride the fire!"

Flames danced off Charro's back, igniting her hooves in flame. The fire spread into her eyes, and steam was released from her nostrils. Two by two, the wheels burst into flames. Charro rocketed up the hill.

"Hold me!" Sergeant Tinison pleaded, holding on for dear life, his legs streaming behind him. "Lords of the Air, please hold me!"

Razor and Bowbreaker grabbed ahold of Tinison.

"We have you!" Razor said.

Ranks of soldiers gathered at the top of the hill. They lowered their spears and lances, forming a deadly barricade.

"Can she get through that?" Zora asked.

"This is the first time I've done this. We're about to find out!" Crane hunkered down. "Hold on!"

Charro thundered ahead. The horses atop the hill stomped their hooves, bucked like mules, and reared. The soldiers fought against the beasts. Some horses bolted. Others snorted and stayed. Charro blasted through them like a flaming battering ram.

Soldiers skipped off the top of the wagon's cage and flipped head over heels. They landed face-first, eating dirt and dust.

"That's it, Charro! Yah!" Crane flipped the whip. Charro thundered down the road, gaining steam.

"They're still coming!" Razor stated.

Scores of riders came from all directions in relentless pursuit. They had no intention of letting the company escape.

"How long can Charro keep this up?" Zora asked.

Crane shrugged. "I don't know, but try not to worry so much."

The prisoner wagon jetted down the hill toward the wharf where the company had docked earlier in the day. The frightened people saw them coming and scattered in all directions. On the far side of the wharf, more soldiers gathered. The well-organized army came from everywhere.

"Lords of Thunder, they're thicker than fire ants!" Shannon said. "How will we escape them all?"

Charro slowed to a stop on the wharf.

The army closed in on both sides.

"Crane, what's happening? Why did she stop?" Zora asked.

"I think she's tired," he said.

Charro snorted.

"Easy, girl. Easy."

Charro snorted again.

"Do something, Crane, or we're all going to become the queen's pincushions!" Razor said.

"Come now, Charro. How about one last ride?" Crane asked. "For me?"

Charro shook her head.

"Seriously, I don't know what's wrong." He looked at Zora. "Maybe now would be a good time to call the dragons."

24

CHARRO SNORTED OUT STEAM. Her burning hooves pawed the wharf. She towed the wagon in a slow circle, shook her head, and whinnied.

"What is she doing?" Zora asked Crane.

"I don't know. She has a mind of her own, like a wild stallion." He tugged on the reins. "Charro, we need to depart. We need to depart now."

Tatiana clutched the Star of Light to her chest, closed her eyes, and chanted quietly.

Sergeant Tinison climbed into the cage. "Pardon me, but am I the only one who sees a thousand soldiers out there?" He scratched his forehead. "I knew I shouldn't have signed up for this."

Zora checked the bright-blue sky. The perfect day showed no sign of dragons.

"Surrender!" a commanding voice called out. It was the same elven sentry that had addressed them earlier. "You have nowhere to run now!"

The Golden Sentries had them pinned in on the south side, and the Black Guards sealed off the north. The Great Basin created a natural barrier in the east, and countless soldiers from the Black Guard crammed any passage to escape to the west.

"Archers!" the Golden Sentry commander said.

"If we don't surrender, they're going to fill us with feathers till we look like chickens," Tinison said.

"Finally, someone has enough sense to think like me," Razor added.

"Tatiana," Zora said in a worried voice. "I don't see any dragons."

The elven sorceress opened her eyes. "Well, Anya didn't make any promises. If she isn't close, there's nothing she can do."

"Aim!" the elven commander said.

Crane snapped his fingers. "I think I might know what the problem is." He reached under his seat and grabbed a burlap sack. He pulled out a juicy plum the size of his fist. "She hasn't had her treat today. It makes her cranky." He tossed the plum to Charro.

She swallowed it whole and opened her mouth again, awaiting another.

"That's it? She's hungry?" Zora asked.

Crane tossed Charro two more. She chomped them down.

"That should do it!"

Charro's hooves burned brighter, as did the fire in her eyes. The flaming wagon wheels spun in a smoky burnout. The burning wheels screamed. The smoke thickened, and Zora could barely make out her hand in front of her face.

"Everyone, grab ahold of something!" Crane shouted.

"Archers, loose!" the elven commander ordered.

The prisoner wagon took off as if shot from a sling. Zora rolled into the back and piled up with the others. They burst out of the ball of smoke.

Arrows sailed through the smoke and struck many Black Guard on the other side.

With his face crammed against the steel bars, Razor said, "Did you see that? They shot themselves!"

Zora fought her way out of the pile of her comrades' bodies. She expected to see Charro plowing through the barricade of men. Instead, she saw something far more horrifying. They rumbled down a long pier that led straight to the basin's water. Local fishermen dropped their rods, scrambled out of their path, and dove into the waters.

"Crane, what in the Flaming Fence are you doing?"

"What's the matter, Zora? Don't you like to swim?"

"No!"

Charro crashed through the wooden railing on the edge of the pier. Hunks of lumber were blasted into pieces.

Everyone screamed as they sailed out over the water. "Aaaaah!"

Sergeant Tinison howled the loudest, "Auuuuuuuuu-uugh! We're going to die! Auuuuuugh!"

Zora's life flashed before her eyes. She saw Grey Cloak, Dyphestive, and Tanlin. Somehow she glanced back at Bowbreaker. "I can't believe it. After all this, I'm going to drown."

"No, you aren't," Crane stated.

The prisoner wagon splashed onto the water and kept going like it was on a perfectly paved roadway. Steam came up from where the water hit the flaming wheels and sizzled. A strong wake followed after them as they sped through the basin like a small craft behind a powerful gust of wind.

Water sprayed Talon's taut faces. Slowly, one by one, their distraught expressions broke into healthy grins.

Razor waved at the bewildered onlookers on a fishing boat. "Now I've seen it all."

Sergeant Tinison stood with his hands on his knees, panting.

Zora caught her breath. "Crane, if these bars didn't stop me, I'd kiss you!"

"Well, who am I to let a little steel get between me and you?" He snapped his fingers. The bars disappeared. He handed the horse whip to Shannon. "Pucker up, little lady!"

"Don't get any grand ideas." And Zora kissed him.

Crane melted back into his seat with his stubby fingers clutched over his heart. "That was worth the wait." He took back the horse whip and cracked it in the air. "Take us somewhere safe, Charro."

With the speed of a dragon, they cruised north across the basin, underneath the last bridge, and up the Great River, leaving their enemies swallowing the bitter water in their wake.

25

THE PAST

THEY SAW no sign of Streak inside the wormholes of tunnels below the surface. Grey Cloak felt a pang in his gut. The longer they walked, the worse it became. Using a small burning tip of the Rod of Weapons for light, he led the way through endless passages.

"I think we've been this way." Zanna had been quiet on the journey, saying little, while Dyphestive remained solemn. "Perhaps this isn't where he came. You might be looking too hard."

"I'm not looking too hard." He didn't want to admit they were in the same spot they'd passed through before. "I know he's down here. We're overlooking something."

Zanna nodded. "If you insist."

"I do."

The trio had been walking longer than Grey Cloak

could keep track of. The only footprints they'd found had come from running across their own. High and low, the walls were rock and dirt. In some places, wispy roots grew from above. No breeze cleared the rotten smell of death that came from the lurker they'd slain earlier.

Grey Cloak jabbed the rod into the wall. "This doesn't make any sense. You said the lurker is a guardian. A guardian of what?"

"Let me correct myself. It could be a guardian," Zanna replied. "I'd assume that since the lurker is dead, its handlers will come to investigate. It might be a wild lurker, living on its own. Perhaps we should separate."

He rolled his eyes. "No. It's hard enough trying to remember our way through this nest."

"I think we should stop." Dyphestive's suggestion drew a hard look from Grey Cloak. "Hear me out. If the lurker does have handlers, perhaps our presence is spooking them, or it—whatever it may be."

"I'm not one for being idle," he replied.

"I think it's a sound suggestion," Zanna agreed. "We've wasted several hours. What's a few more?"

"Did you ever stop to think Streak might not have a few hours?"

"I have," she said, "but we aren't getting anywhere. Now might be the best time to exercise more patience as opposed to stumbling blindly through these tunnels."

Grey Cloak pulled his rod out of the wall. "Two hours, not a moment more. Let's find a good place to hide."

They backtracked toward the pit where they'd killed the lurker. Once they spread out, they hid within the corridor's natural nooks. Grey Cloak doused the rod's light and wrapped up in his cloak. The quiet and pitch-blackness eased his senses.

He allowed himself to breathe. The stillness gave him time to think over matters. His mother, Zanna, left him perplexed, and she gave him little comfort. He wanted to trust her but couldn't fully commit. Something about her ate at him.

Her arrival, though reasonably explained, is all too convenient. Of course, Dyphestive trusts her, but what does he know?

He set his thoughts aside and focused on Streak. His heart clenched at the thought of losing his dragon. If something happened to Streak, he would never forgive himself.

Time passed. The earthen tunnels were so quiet, he couldn't even hear his friends breathing.

I'm surprised Dyphestive isn't snoring, but I think it's time we wrapped up this pointless assignment. Zooks, this talking in my head is becoming irritating.

Grey Cloak started to emerge from his hiding spot. A faint scuffle caught his ear. It was so soft and gentle that it was virtually undetectable. Whatever it was, it didn't move on human feet, or hooves, for that matter. It moved solidly enough to disturb the dirt beneath it.

At first, Grey Cloak hoped it might be Streak finding his way back, but his veins iced up. A foreboding presence tickled the marrow inside his bones. Peeking through his hood, he could make out a dark blot coming his way.

Great Gapoli, what is that?

The creature's shape began to take form. It appeared to be a great spider, no bigger than a man, walking on eight bony legs, carrying a larger body built like a man. More than one marched down the tunnel.

Zooks!

He watched in horror as a train of odd creatures marched by him. His muscles wanted to burst from his skin. He pressed deeper into the cleft. At close range, his keen eyes took in their shapes fully.

They're part spider and part man! Abominable!

The numerous strange creatures walked slowly by on spider legs.

Grey Cloak had read about centaurs, but he'd never read about creatures like this before.

Finally, the train of monsters passed and moved deeper toward the lurker pit, rounding the bend and disappearing from sight.

Grey Cloak detached from his hiding spot, rubbing his body like thousands of spiders were crawling all over him. He ignited the rod's tip.

Dyphestive and Zanna emerged.

"Did you see those nasty things? I didn't get a close

look, but I didn't want to." He looked at Zanna. "What were they?"

"I have no idea." She rubbed the goose bumps on her arms. "And that scares me."

He slapped his brother on the chest. "Well done. Your plan worked, and we drew them out. They must have Streak." He pointed down the tunnel. "And we're going to find him." He didn't take two steps before Zanna grabbed him. "What are you—"

She clamped her hand over his mouth and whispered, "They're coming back. Hide."

26

THE WEIRD SPIDER people's trail was anything but easy to follow. They moved quickly and quietly. Grey Cloak remained focused. He knew Streak was down there somewhere.

Whatever these foul creatures are, they will lead me to him.

He picked up the pace, checking backward from time to time, making sure Dyphestive and Zanna kept up and didn't get lost. The blue tip of his rod burned like an ember from a fire, showing light but giving off little illumination.

Faint impressions spaced uniformly on the cave floor would have been undetectable to the naked eye. Grey Cloak picked up on the spider people's patters. They made a trail but uniquely covered it up at the same time. Light of foot on the fine hairs of their spidery legs, they were no easier to track than insects. But Grey Cloak was determined.

After a long and arduous trek, Grey Cloak came to a stop. He fed a little more light into the rod and swept the tip over the ground. The monsters' tracks came to a dead end.

"No," he moaned, searching the area frantically.

"What is it?" Dyphestive whispered.

"Stay still, please." He followed the trail back a dozen feet, passing Zanna as he did so, and came back to the dead end. "They vanished. It's not possible." He fought to keep his temper in check. He wanted to smash something. *Don't lose your head. You have to keep your head for Streak's sake.*

Zanna squatted down and put her fingers in the dirt. "This is Dyphestive's footprint. I thought this passage looked familiar. We passed through it earlier."

The tunnel's walls were as solid as a tombstone. No cracks or crevices or breaks in the wall allowed other critters to pass through.

Grey Cloak poked the rod hard into the wall. Chunks of dirt came down. "There must be a secret passage somewhere. How else would they disappear?"

"I say we continue in the direction we're going," Zanna suggested. "Certainly, we'll pick up the trail farther down."

"Agreed," Dyphestive said. "Don't lose hope, brother."

"Who's losing hope?" His voice carried. "Sorry. I only want to find my dragon."

"We all do. We will," Zanna assured him. She reached for the rod. "Would you like me to take the lead?"

He brought the rod back to his chest, started to shake his head, gave in, and offered it to Zanna. "Yes, take it. My eyes could use the—" His skin prickled all over like a thousand eyes were watching him. His eyes met Zanna's then Dyphestive's. "Don't look up."

Dyphestive's chin started to rise.

"I said don't!" he whispered.

A presence lurked above him.

The Cloak of Legends warmed.

"Follow my lead and resume the search." He lowered the rod toward the ground and swept its glowing tip over the floor.

Dyphestive and Zanna continued down the passage, their hands dusting over the walls.

If something indeed was watching them, Grey Cloak didn't want to spook it. He needed the element of surprise and glanced casually upward. He spotted a blot in the rocks, and he swore he saw the face of a man. He crept away from it, summoned more wizard fire, turned, and fired a blast into the ceiling.

The ceiling moved.

A streak of blue energy shot into the blur of motion. It hit with a crack and a sizzle. A body fell from above and landed flat on its back. The spider person flipped onto its legs and turned to run.

Grey Cloak unleashed two more balls of energy into the monster.

Bzzztuu! Bzzztuu!

It screeched, spasmed hard, and collapsed.

He poked it with the rod. It no longer moved.

Dyphestive rushed over. "Did you kill it?"

"I think so." Grey Cloak fully illuminated the staff. "Ick. That thing is creepy."

The arachnid person was a little smaller than a human. Its insectoid body was colored in broad black and yellow stripes. It had the torso of a person and huge eyes like black marbles. Two small antennae protruded from the top of its head, and a gooey, weblike saliva oozed from its mouth to the ground.

"I know I've never read about them in the ancient annals," Grey Cloak said.

"Me either," replied Zanna. "This is disconcerting."

Grey Cloak lifted his light toward the ceiling. Another passage opened high above them. "Now we know why we were walking in circles. Come on. It's time to climb."

It didn't take Grey Cloak long to find the spider people's tracks again. He followed their path the same as before into another network of underground tunnels. He moved with renewed purpose and determination.

An unusual moaning started inside the tunnel. The farther they went, the louder it became. He shared some concerned glances with his family and slowed his pace. A warm yellow light shone down the next twist in the tunnel. A larger passageway opened up.

Grey Cloak doused his light. They walked down the long passage. Spider people scurried across the floor at the end of the passage and disappeared in what appeared to be a larger chamber.

"We aren't going that way." Grey Cloak spotted a smaller passage that split off from the main one. He took it. "Follow me."

The passage had a low ceiling. They crouched down and hurried toward the light. At the end, an overlook showed a scene unlike anything they'd ever viewed. A huge pocket in the earth opened up. The cavernous place was filled with more spider people than Grey Cloak could count. Gigantic spiderwebs stretched as far as the eye could see. Ropes of webbing crisscrossed all over. Cocoon-like sacks attached to the ceiling with webs hung by the dozens. Bodies wriggled like worms inside some.

Grey Cloak shook off a frightened chill and slunk back to his comrades. "Any ideas?"

The stunned looks on their faces said it all.

"No worries. I'll think of something." He crawled back to the overlook and stared out over the vast, creepy, crawling chambers. "But suggestions are welcome."

27

ZANNA HOVERED over Grey Cloak's shoulder. "Those arachnamen won't be easy to slip past."

"Arachnamen?" His eyes swept the area. "A fitting name. Why don't we walk out there and introduce ourselves? Perhaps they will lead us to our dragon."

"No need to be sarcastic. It's only a name," she said.

The arachnamen spoke in their own bubbly alien tongue, accompanied by a series of hoots and other odd sounds. They moved like worker ants along their sticky ropes, crossing over the expanse and vanishing into smaller wormholes in the earth.

One of the arachnamen walked on a spiderweb, grabbed a cocoon, stuck it on his back, and headed down toward a blanket of webbing at the bottom. He plucked the cocoon off his back and dropped it through a gap in the webbing. Another arachnaman appeared under the webbing, grabbed the cocoon, and vanished into a black pit.

"That's not good." Grey Cloak squinted. Horror overtook him. "This chamber has no floor." He pointed. "Look."

The chamber's walls slid down into a pit that could swallow twenty horses stretched end to end.

"I hope we don't have to go down there," Dyphestive said. "It looks deep. Like a monstrous well."

"No doubt," Grey Cloak said. "Well, I for one think we've gone deep enough. Look for Streak. He has to be here somewhere."

The cocoons varied in size, as did the arachnamen. A few of the arachnamen appeared bigger than horses. Others were small, like halflings, but most of them were little bigger than humans.

Zanna patted Grey Cloak's shoulder. "Look there." She pointed at a nearby cocoon.

The round face of a tiny woman pressed against the thin strands of webbing, her eyes wide open. Her lips moved, as if she were pleading.

"That's a halfling. Even if we find Streak, we can't abandon them," she said.

"*If* we find Streak?"

"You know what I meant. We can't leave these people hanging."

"Haha, but one rescue at a time. As unfortunate as their

situation is, Streak is the priority." His gaze swept over every cocoon one by one. The glowing minerals on the chamber's walls made for poor lighting, especially on the cocoons toward the middle. The walls of webbing scattered throughout the chamber blocked the view of many cocoons on the other side. "I need to get a closer look."

Zanna held him back. "What do you plan to do, walk to the other side? They'll see you."

"I have to risk it. Don't worry. I'll be careful. Besides, I think the *arachnamen* are distracted with their work." He watched another arachnaman carry a cocoon toward the deep. "We can't wait for Streak to be taken down there. He's here. I'll find him."

"Be careful," his mother said.

"That goes without saying. Bye now." He slipped the Scarf of Shadows over his nose and vanished.

"He's a fearless little mongrel, isn't he?" Zanna asked Dyphestive.

"The best. When the Doom Riders captured me, he didn't rest until he found me. If not for him, I'd be lost. His loyalty saved me." Dyphestive squeezed Zanna's shoulder. "He comes from good stock."

She touched his hand. "You both do, but I wasn't as brave as he is when I was your age. I know that much." Her pride mixed with guilt. "Do you think he'll ever forgive me?"

"For what?"

"Not being there when he was a child."

"I'd say he's forgiven you already, but don't expect to hear those words. He can be hardheaded."

"Yes, he gets that from his mother too."

Grey Cloak moved quickly. He climbed to the higher ledges of the cavern, getting a closer look at the cocoons. The more he saw, the worse his stomach twisted. Trapped inside the cocoons' webbing were faces frozen in anguish. The bodies twinged from time to time. Staring at one cocoon, he swore the person within saw him. Their eyes pleaded desperately.

The arachnamen feasted on them far, far below. They were being harvested.

An entire horse was stored inside one cocoon. Its legs kicked every so often. The strand of webbing it hung from flexed, and its body bounced on the strand.

This is sick. They're eating people—or something is. Oh my.

On the other side of the chamber hung the largest cocoon of all. There was no mistaking the broad face wrapped within.

A giant. Zooks. They captured a giant.

Grey Cloak moved along the ledge and positioned himself for a closer look. The giant balled up inside the webbing must have stood at least twelve feet tall at one time. Now, cradled in a blanket of death, it didn't move. A long braid of fiery-red hair protruded from the webbing.

He's a her.

The only giant he'd met before was Tontor at Lake Flugen's shores. He still owed Tontor a vat of butter. He'd never imagined a female. The mere thought of the arachnamen taking down a giant sent chills through his bones.

He caught a quiver of movement out of the corner of his eye. He turned to look over his shoulder. A small dragon wing stuck out of a cocoon. *Streak!*

The suspended cocoon hung near the middle of the chamber. He had only one way to reach it. Grey Cloak would have to walk the tightrope of web cords that crossed from one side to the other. He stepped down and grabbed the cord. It was sticky, but his hand could still come free.

I can do this. He started walking up the tightrope of webbing.

On the other side of the rope, an arachnaman stopped his journey, turned, and came right at Grey Cloak.

Zooks! How can it see me?

28

THE ARACHNAMAN CAME DOWN the narrow rope of webbing as if walking on flat ground. Its thin legs switched back and forth on the rope. The arachnaman stopped a few dozen feet away. It carried a small spear in its tiny man hands. Its dark, sorcerous eyes stared down the line straight at Grey Cloak.

Does he see me or not?

When the arachnaman moved, the webbing underfoot vibrated.

Ah, it doesn't see me. It felt me.

Bubbles of webbing spit out of the arachnaman's mouth and floated toward Grey Cloak.

What's this? Disgusting.

The bubble floated within a foot of Grey Cloak and

started to fall away before sticking to the strands of webbing below. The arachnaman stared through Grey Cloak one last time then moved up the rope and leapt to another.

The webbing shifted under Grey Cloak's feet. He lost his balance and fell. He stretched out his fingers and caught the webbing in one hand while holding the Rod of Weapons in the other. He hung by two fingers, suspended over a giant web waiting to catch him below.

This would be much easier if I could see myself.

He kicked his legs back and forth. Gaining momentum, he launched into the air, did a backflip, and landed tiptoe on the rope of web where he'd started. Shifting his arms in the air, and using the staff, he fought to keep his balance.

Whew!

One foot after the other, he crossed slim bridges of webbing until he faced Streak at eye level. "Ah, look at you," he said quietly.

Streak was bundled up like a ball of twine with his nose and tail tucked into his body.

Grey Cloak lay his hand on the sticky cotton-like shell of the cocoon. He pressed his hand into it. He felt Streak's heartbeat against his palm. *Thank goodness you're alive. Now, how am I going to get you out of here?*

Arachnamen scurried high and low inside the chamber, but their numbers were thinning. Most of them disappeared into the wormholes while a worker lowered another cocoon into the throat of the black hole.

Finding his bearings, Grey Cloak spotted the overlook where Dyphestive and Zanna waited. He could make out the crown of Dyphestive's head as he stared into the sticky abyss.

I need to get their attention.

He gave the cocoon a gentle push, hoping the feeble effort wouldn't disrupt the Scarf of Shadows' powers. Hanging from the strand of webbing, Streak's cocoon swung like a pendulum.

Zanna's head twisted around. She nudged Dyphestive and pointed at the cocoon.

"Do you see that?" Zanna asked. "That cocoon is moving, and I swear that's Streak's wing."

"You have good eyes. I didn't notice that." Dyphestive adjusted his position and looked up at the cocoon. "See how the webbing bows? Do you think Grey Cloak is standing there?"

"Good eyes, yourself. Impressive," she said.

The cocoon stopped swinging and started again a moment later.

"I think he's trying to send us a message," Dyphestive said.

"If we could only read his mind. If you were Grey Cloak, what would you do in this situation?" she asked.

Dyphestive's head bobbed. "I'd snatch Streak's cocoon and run for it." He reached back and grabbed his sword. "I have a feeling we better get ready."

A blue light flared where Grey Cloak stood. His entire body reappeared. He started cutting Streak free.

"Spoken like a sage," Zanna said.

Dyphestive scrutinized the chamber of webs. Arachnamen crept along the walls and webs from top to bottom, but he only spotted a cluster of them spread out in the chamber.

He watched Grey Cloak slink across the webs. "Hurry, brother, hurry."

The wizard fire ate away the cocoon's webbing. Grey Cloak pulled the dragon out of the shell and clutched him tight. "I have you, brother."

Streak yawned and looked down. "If you've got me, who has you?"

"Shhh, keep your voice down." He crept ever so slowly across the webbing. "I don't want to alert the arachnamen."

"The arachna-what?"

Grey Cloak pinched the dragon's snout shut. With his enemies' eyes looking the other way, he picked up the pace.

Almost there. Almost there.

An arachnaman popped out of a wormhole above and adjacent to his position. He froze in place. The vile creature scurried up the wall and vanished into the darkness of the ceiling. His heart thumped, and he resumed walking toward the overlook. Dyphestive and Zanna silently waved him on.

This would be much easier if I were invisible.

After a quick glance up and down to ensure the coast was clear, Grey Cloak jumped down toward the overlook. He floated down at an agonizing pace until his toe touched the lip of the overhang.

Dyphestive grabbed his cloak and hauled him inside. He hugged his brother, crushing Streak between them. "You did it, brother. You did it."

"Easy, brother. You're breaking our backs."

"You can say that again," Streak said.

"Sorry." Dyphestive released his embrace and rubbed Streak's head. "It's good to see you again. What happened?"

"I don't know. One moment I was soaring the skies, minding my own business. Then I saw something bright and shiny, and everything got a little fuzzy after that. That cocoon was warm and cozy, however."

"I'm sure whatever was going to eat you wanted to keep your blood warm," Zanna replied.

"Ew. You make it sound so inhumane. Maybe I should start cooking my prey before I eat it," the runt dragon said.

The strange moaning made by the arachnamen continued, covering the sound of their voices.

"Now that we're safe, it's time to leave," Grey Cloak said.

Zanna stood with her arms crossed, peering over the overlook. "Did you forget about them?"

"No," Grey Cloak said, "but I was hoping you would."

29

"Do you see that oversized cocoon?" Grey Cloak pointed. "That one is a giant, a lady giant. She's more than twice our size. How do you expect to move her out of there?"

Zanna pulled a knife from her bracer. "I'll cut her down."

"And let her fall into that abyss?"

"I'm jesting." Zanna slid the blade back into her bracer's sheath. "I didn't say it would be easy, only that it needs to be done."

Grey Cloak sighed. Zanna wasn't in charge. He was. He needed to put her in her place. "Aren't you the one insisting we lie low?"

"We are low." Zanna took out a scroll stuck in her boot.

"And I don't think we can get any lower. No one will remember what happens down here."

"The people we save will."

"Boss, if I may interject," Streak said, "I don't think those people want to go like that. I've seen what those arachnamen do. They feed on the people." His scales shivered, and the black stripes on his back waved up and down. "Suck the blood right out of them. It's an awful sound."

"How morbid." Dyphestive's face turned sour. "We have to save these people."

"We have to save ourselves."

"You're the one who insisted on staying out of the tower. These are the consequences," Zanna reminded him.

He got in Zanna's face. "And if we were in the towers, it wouldn't make any difference, would it?"

"But we're here now."

"Great." Grey Cloak hadn't gained any ground. "If we all wind up in one of those cocoons, it's on you." He looked at the scroll in Zanna's hand. "What do you have in mind?"

"A distraction." She wiggled the scroll under Grey Cloak's nose. "If we can trick the arachnamen into leaving their hives, we can use that time to free the others. No guarantees that they'll make it out alive, but at least we'll have tried."

He offered a nod. "I can live with that. Let's see what you have planned."

"Stand back." Zanna unrolled the scroll. "And don't interrupt me."

With Streak in his arms, Grey Cloak joined Dyphestive.

"You made the right choice, brother," Dyphestive said.

"That's easy to say when you're still alive."

Zanna's dark-red lips moved as she murmured a chant. Her lovely eyes captured the light from the golden illumination cast by the scroll. A chill breeze stirred their hair and clothing. The scroll turned brittle in Zanna's hand and crumbled into ashes.

Grey Cloak rubbed the back of his neck. "Interesting." He stood on the overlook. "Everything seems to be in order. The arachnamen are going about their business. Ah, look, they're lowering another cocoon into the abyss." He faced the group. "Well done, Mother. You've outdone yourself."

Zanna dusted off her hands. "It will be a few moments." She looked at Dyphestive. "Is his tongue always so sharp?"

"Only on his good days... and bad ones."

She laughed quietly.

Grey Cloak turned his back, crossed his arms, and leaned against the wall. He watched the hive. *This is madness. She's going to get us all killed. Not that I mind rescuing strangers, but at what cost? I saved Streak, and that should be the end of it. What about the bigger mission? Do we have to save every unfortunate creature before we save the rest of the world?*

Dirt began to fall from the ceiling above Grey Cloak. He leaned back, dusting the grit from his shoulders. A head popped out of the dirt. Grey Cloak pointed a dagger at the creature's nose. It stuck its tongue out at him.

"What is that thing?"

Zanna pushed his hand down. "Easy. Those are the gremlins I summoned."

"Gremlins?" he asked.

Another gremlin popped its head out of the dirt by Zanna's feet. Several of them popped out all over and clawed their way out of the ground. They were bigger than groundhogs, ugly-faced with strong pointed features, and had bumpy skin like toads. They had four claws for hands and feet and moved like little men.

Zanna knelt and spoke to them in a language Grey Cloak didn't understand. The brothers exchanged disconcerted looks. The gremlins nodded, hissed, and scratched behind their big ears, using their legs like dogs. One of them scratched his butt, while another picked a gooey substance from his wide nostril.

She led them to the overlook and pointed at the arachnamen. Where she pointed, the gremlins pointed. One of them climbed up her back like a monkey and stood on her head. It held its taloned hand over its eyes like a sailor on the lookout.

"I'm glad you're keeping close contact with your friends," Grey Cloak stated. "Will they be joining us for the rest of our journey?"

"Perhaps."

The gremlin on her head spoke to the others with short, quick, incomprehensible words. It leapt into the hive. The others followed. In the wink of an eye, a score of gremlins spread out and traversed the webbing like squirrels. They shook the ropes of web bridges and swung on the suspended cocoons. They screeched like wild children and beat their little chests like jungle beasts.

"Here we go." Zanna smirked.

The arachnamen went rigid. Their strange moaning stopped. They turned their eyes to their new enemies swinging from web to web like spider monkeys. Their antennas bent downward, and they chased after the gremlins.

30

THE GREMLINS MADE the quick-footed arachnamen look like ogres chasing squirrels. The arachnamen charged full speed only to watch the gremlins spring away at the last second. Sticking out their long tongues and wiggling their fingers, their thumbs stuffed in their earholes, the gremlins taunted the alien spider creatures.

Bubbles of webbing sprayed from the arachnamen's mouths, catching one careless gremlin hanging from a web vine, doing a loop the loop. The gooey orbs clung to his body, slowing his acrobatics and sticking him to the vine.

A pair of arachnamen pounced. Strands of webbing shot from the spinnerets on their thoraxes. They quickly balled up the gremlin in silky thread and hung him like an ornament.

The wide-eyed gremlins shrieked like wild monkeys.

They scattered like flies and made a break for the wormholes. Every arachnaman gave chase, some with spears in hand and others without. All of them vanished into the surrounding tunnels and wormholes and were gone.

The arachnamen's moaning and hooting vanished as well. Aside from the dangling cocoons of death, the hive was abandoned.

"Let's go." Zanna moved to the end of the overlook and took her place on a stretch of webbing. Her boots clung to the rope, but she could walk. "This is nasty."

As Grey Cloak joined her, Dyphestive asked, "What do you want me to do?"

"Keep your ears peeled, and we'll send the rescues to you."

Streak perched on the ledge and spread his wings. "I can help." He launched into the air, taking flight, while carefully maneuvering through the obstacles. Using his claws and fire, he opened one cocoon after another.

Zanna ignited a dagger with wizard fire. She cut into the strands like a hot knife through butter. Grey Cloak did the same. Using the Rod of Weapons, he ignited the blue tip, sliced a cocoon open, and peeled it away. He caught a halfling in his arms.

The little man sputtered and gasped. Spittle dripped down his chin. "Thank you. Mercy me, thank you."

"Can you climb?" Grey Cloak asked.

"You bet. I'll dig my way out of here if I have to," the bright-eyed halfling said.

Grey Cloak pointed at Dyphestive, who was waving. "Go to him. Hurry."

The halfling fought his way across the sticky web vines, a desperate look in his eyes. More halflings joined him, crawling at an agonizing pace toward Dyphestive.

"This is going to take forever," Grey Cloak said to Zanna, who stood a few web bridges above him. "They move like they're in a daze."

"Gum up and keep sawing," she said.

"You gum up."

Over half a score of not-so-able-bodied halflings climbed toward the overlook. Dyphestive had only hauled a few of them into the tunnel. Many others were stuck on the webbing, dangling by their hands and feet. One woman hung upside down. The blurry-eyed woman started wailing like a wounded calf.

"Zooks! Tell her to gum up!" Grey Cloak practically spit.

"I'll handle it. At least they're all halflings." Zanna jumped from one web vine to another and lifted the little woman into her arms.

"This is madness." He made his way over to the giant woman. She was balled in the fetal position, and her eyes were closed. She looked dead, but he could feel her heartbeat through the cocoon. "Here goes. I hope this doesn't come back to bite me." He started sawing her out.

"No, no!" the first halfling man he'd rescued shouted from the overlook. "Don't free her. She's evil! Let the giant face her fate!"

The cocoon split open. The giant's limbs loosened, and her big brown eyes opened wide.

"Hello."

The giant fastened her eyes on Grey Cloak. Her wooly eyebrows buckled. She let out an angry growl and swiped at him.

He jumped away. "Zanna, this one is on her own!"

The giant tore her body out of her cocoon. She was stalwart, brawny from head to toe, and dressed in a warrior's leather armor, bracers, and boots.

"Get away from her! She'll eat you!" the halfling with Dyphestive shouted.

Dyphestive clamped his hand over the little man's face. "Pipe down."

"Grrrrrrr," the giant woman growled. She clawed at the network of web vines that supported her body. Many of them broke against her strength, and she plummeted deeper into the hive.

Out of the corner of his eye, Grey Cloak spotted a group of arachnamen coming back through the wormholes. "Zanna! We have company!"

Zanna stood on a web vine, picked up a halfling by his clothing, and shouted, "Dyphestive, catch!" She tossed the halfling like a bale of hay.

Dyphestive caught the little man softly in his arms. She tossed two more down.

Spears in hand, a quartet of arachnamen scurried down the web vines.

More halflings screamed, but the last of them made it into the overlook.

Hooked to a strand of webbing, the arachnamen dropped down from their threads like spiders. They surrounded Zanna and blew gooey bubbles from their mouths. Twin blades appeared in her hands. Their blue tips burned like flames.

Jab! Jab! Jab! Jab!

Zanna's strikes ate through the webbing. Steel lanced deep into insect chests. Arachnamen hung dead in the very spot they set their trap.

"Grey Cloak, Streak, we need to get out of here!" Zanna said.

"You think?" Streak weaved his way through the webbing. "No need to tell me twice. I've seen enough."

Grey Cloak didn't wait around either. He climbed toward the overlook. Below him, the giant fell deeper into the hive. She landed on the bed of webbing at the bottom. She wiggled and strained against the adhesive bonds but could not break free.

When her eyes met his, he found humanity in them, and she pleaded for her life, "Please, help me!"

He was almost to the overlook. Dyphestive reached

down.

The giant screamed again. “Help! Help!”

Grey Cloak looked at his brother. “I can’t believe I’m doing this. Get those halflings out of here, brother.”

“But—”

“Go!” Grey Cloak looked down at the giant and jumped.

31

Grey Cloak floated down and landed on the web by the giant. She thrashed like a trapped bear.

"Be still," he ordered her.

The webbing had firmly tangled her hands and arms. He started sawing it away with the rod.

"Thank you," she said in a deep, womanly voice.

"Don't thank me yet." He cut away more webs, opening up a gap that dropped into the black hole. "If this web gives, we'll both be swallowed whole."

"I'm Breen."

"Grey Cloak is my name. Doing foolish things is my game." He cut enough away to where she could sit up. "That ought to do it. Can you stand?"

Breen clumsily fought her way to her feet. The web wobbled beneath her. She stuck out her arms for balance.

"What do you say we get out of here, Breen?"

"You don't have to tell me twice." She marched toward the hive wall covered in frosty webbing. She planted her hands in the dirt of the wall and started to climb.

"Impressive." The coast was clear, and he took a breath. "We're going to make it after all."

"Hoot! Hoot! Hoot! Hoot! Hoot! Hoot!"

The sound came from the bottomless pit.

Dyphestive peeked over the ledge. "Are those owls?"

Grey Cloak looked down. Icy fingers clawed down his back.

Zooks!

Arachnamen streamed out of the hole by the dozens.

"Hoot! Hoot! Hoot! Hoot! Hoot! Hoot!"

"Breen! Climb faster!"

She glanced down, and her pretty brown eyes grew like flowers. Her big body scaled the wall like a mountaineer. She hit the overlook and crammed herself into the tunnel.

Grey Cloak was right behind her. He pushed her rear end in farther. "Go! Go! Go!"

He took one last look down, and his jaw dropped. The arachnamen came, but so did something bigger. Giant spider legs emerged from the black hole and pierced the hive's wall. It dwarfed any arachnaman by comparison. The gigantic, beastly, horrific arachnawoman could swallow the likes of Breen whole.

"Dirty chipmunks, that must be the queen," he muttered.

Breen low-crawled through the hole. Her body blocked Grey Cloak's passage. He kicked her rear end. "How'd they get you down here anyway?"

"I don't know. And stop poking me, little one."

Arachnamen entered the tunnel. Grey Cloak turned the Rod of Weapons on them. Balls of blue energy streaked into three separate bodies, sending them scurrying away. Three more entered the gap. He fired again, hitting two full in the chest and searing their bodies. They kept coming.

He unloaded. "Aaaaaaaaaaah!"

Forces of energy blasted the arachnamen into bits and pieces, arms, legs, and antennae flying everywhere. One arachnaman opened his mouth wide and spewed bubbles. He swallowed a ball of energy, and his face exploded.

Streak stood by Grey Cloak's feet. "Nice work, but we need to go."

Grey Cloak's chest heaved. The tip of his rod smoked. The way behind him was clear. "After you," he gasped.

Streak scurried across the tunnel floor with Grey Cloak on his tail. They entered the broader passage and gained on Breen.

Two arachnamen stepped into the giant woman's path. She kicked one of them down the tunnel, grabbed the second one, and smashed it like a bug on the wall. It popped against the rocks, and green bug ooze squirted out of its body.

"Keep going! Keep going!" Grey Cloak hollered.

The passage narrowed ahead. Breen turned sideways and squeezed into the crevice.

Grey Cloak caught up with her and thought better of pushing her through. A surge of arachnamen came. "Inhale, woman! It will make you skinny!"

"I don't know that I care for that remark." She sucked in her breath and shimmied through.

Streak stepped in front of Grey Cloak. "I've got this, boss." He blew out a stream of thick smoke, engulfing the tunnel, and backed into the passage.

Grey Cloak scooped up Streak in one arm and walked backward. "Well done, but I've got another idea." He aimed the Rod of Weapons at the ceiling and fired away.

The balls of energy burst like thunderbolts, ripping the ceiling apart. The tunnel crumbled and collapsed. The passage filled up, and dust rolled over them.

They caught up with the others in the spot where they'd killed the lurker. Terrorized halflings scrambled up the walls. Breen picked them up in her arms and tossed them like bundles of hay to Zanna and Dyphestive.

She faced Grey Cloak and extended her arms. "Need a hand?"

"Why not?"

She lifted him and Streak to the top of the hole. They

met the others inside the chasm. The halflings were already on the run.

Breen climbed out of the gap and caught a wink of sun in her eyes. "I never thought I'd see the light again. I thank you!"

The ground trembled beneath their feet.

"Don't thank me yet," Grey Cloak said.

Zanna waved them on. "Hurry, hurry!" She led Dyphestive, Grey Cloak, Streak, and Breen down the chasm toward the awaiting fracture of daylight.

Escape. Grey Cloak could taste the wide fields and open air on the tip of his tongue. "Streak, promise me you won't do anything so foolish again."

"I can't promise that, but I won't chase any more shiny objects into deep pits," the dragon replied.

"We're almost there!" Zanna said.

The company caught up with the short-legged halflings. Dyphestive picked up two winded halflings and ran with them. They could see long fields of green pastures ahead. The insectoid horrors in the deep would shortly become a thing of the past, a memory where nightmares were made.

Jogging backward, Zanna waved them on to open air and freedom as the great channel opened wide. "Onward, to safety."

A cord of webbing hit Zanna in the back and ripped her off her feet. The halflings skidded to a halt, cowered, and screamed. The queen of the arachnamen loomed above the chasm, her great legs stretched from one side to the other. The giant arachnawoman's quick insect legs balled Zanna up like twine, covering her head to toe in webbing. She climbed down onto the ground, blocking passage to the plains.

A wild hooting carried down the channel. The arachnamen came after them like a swarm of rats.

Dyphestive set down the halflings and lifted his sword. "I guess it's not over."

"No." Grey Cloak fired up the Rod of Weapons. "Not by a long shot."

32

"That's one ugly spider," Dyphestive said.

Grey Cloak replied, "That's an understatement."

The arachna-queen stood over two stories tall. She had a rat's nest of stringy hair hanging down and covering most of her body. Big antennae with bulbs on the ends protruded from the top of her skull. Her oversized eyes were bug-green with thousands of tiny eyes within. Unlike the arachnamen, who had two human arms, she had four and stood on six spider legs covered in barbs as long as a man's finger.

"My heart pounds like a drum." Breen pulled a dagger from her belt. As tall as the giant woman was, she didn't make up half the height of the arachna-queen. "Our dwarven enemies have a saying, 'Take the legs, take the head.' Who's with me?"

The arachnamen, big and small, surrounded the company from all sides of the chasm, standing rows deep.

"Easier said than done." Dyphestive glanced up at Breen. "But I like the way you think." Keeping his eyes fixed on the queen, he added, "Hello, I'm Dyphestive."

"Nice to meet you," Breen said in a brutish voice. "A shame the circumstances couldn't be better."

The arachna-queen dropped Zanna's cocoon like a loaf of bread. She opened her mouth, revealing a multitude of sharp teeth, and let out an earsplitting shriek. Grey Cloak's knees buckled. The halflings balled up like wooly worms and clamped their hands over their ears.

Once the queen's shrieking stopped, Grey Cloak rolled his jaw and tugged on his earlobe. "That was awful."

"What do we do, boss?" Streak asked.

Their enemies hadn't attacked. Instead, they remained poised to strike, waiting on their queen's orders. Grey Cloak noticed the queen's eyes locked on the Rod of Weapons's light. He moved it slowly from side to side. Her eyes followed.

"Either she wants the wizard fire, or she fears it." He fed more energy from his body into the rod. The spear tip blossomed.

The arachna-queen's eyes reflected the blue fire. She started to climb up the chasm's walls.

"She fears it. She fears the flame." Grey Cloak moved forward. The queen moved farther up the wall. "I'll be.

Dyphestive, pick up Zanna. Halflings, wake up. We need to move, but slowly."

Grey Cloak positioned himself right underneath the queen. Her huge body made a bridge over him. She looked down at him with thousands of glowering eyes. Sticky ooze dripped from her dreadful mouth. Her breath reeked of rotten flesh, and her long legs lanced the channel's walls.

Man, giant, dragon, and halfling cleared the passage, making it all the way through to the open plains.

"Come on, Grey!" Dyphestive called out with Zanna slung over his shoulder. "We're free! Hurry!"

Grey Cloak backed toward the exit. He kept the rod pointed at the queen. She turned in the gap. Her children crept down the channel. They all moved as one, like fish.

It sent a shiver through Grey Cloak. *I hope I never see these things again.*

Dyphestive called out again. "Hurry!"

From the shadows of the chasm, Grey Cloak started to jog backward. He waved at the queen. "I wish I could say it was a pleasure to meet you, but it wasn't. Go back to your giant hole, uglies!" He turned and ran.

He cleared the chasm and was greeted by the warm sunlight like a kiss from heaven. He drank in the air.

Thwwwwip!

Grey Cloak ducked. A strand of web seized the Rod of Weapons and spun him around. He faced the queen, who'd snagged the rod with a long vine of webbing. She started reeling in Grey Cloak.

He dug his heels into the ground and held onto the rod for dear life. "Dyphestive!" he called as his boots and bottom slid over the grass. "We have a problem!"

"Coming!" Dyphestive dropped Zanna and ran for Grey Cloak.

The halflings sprinted in the opposite direction and vanished over the first rise.

"I'm coming, too, boss, hold on!" Streak said.

Breen came running as well.

Dyphestive jumped down behind Grey Cloak, wrapped his arms around his body, and heaved. Breen did the same thing to Dyphestive. They battled in a tug-of-war with the queen. Their feet skidded forward. The queen was winning.

Grey Cloak's fingers burned and slipped. "Streak!" he yelled. "Cut the cord! Hurry!"

Streak landed by the strand of web. His yellow eyes burned like flames. He took in a lungful of air and spread his wings. Flames shot out of his mouth. The rod slipped free of Grey Cloak's fingers, jettisoning through the dragon fire, and the arachna-queen caught it in her clutches. Grey Cloak's jaw hung.

"A good plan, but missed by a fraction of a second. I hate it when that happens. So, boss." Streak cocked his head and looked at Grey Cloak. "What's plan B?"

“Run!”

33

"TAKE TO THE SKY, STREAK!" Grey Cloak said. "And stay there!"

Streak sprinted through the grass. Spreading his wings, he jumped and took flight. "Aye! Aye!"

Grey Cloak could outrun the arachnamen, but Dyphestive and Breen were another matter. Breen picked up Zanna, but she couldn't run any faster than Dyphestive. They weren't slow by any stretch of the imagination, but they weren't fast enough either. In the end, it didn't matter. The sea of arachnamen caught up with them and encircled them two hundred yards later. They were trapped. Breen set down Zanna. The trio on foot formed a defensive triangle around the cocoon.

Dyphestive cocked his sword over his shoulder. "This is grim. Are you thinking what I'm thinking?"

Grey Cloak produced the Figurine of Heroes. "Yes. How much worse can it get?"

"What is that?" Breen asked.

He set the figurine down in their midst. "Life or death." He sighed. "*Osid-ayan-umra-shokrah-ha!*"

The faceless figurine of a man stood no bigger than the span between his thumb and index finger. Its smooth shiny-black surface reflected the sunlight and began to spout inky-black smoke like a chimney. The plume grew bigger and bigger, covering the heroes and the field of arachnamen. The ground sank under Grey Cloak's feet. He stepped back. Whatever he'd summoned was big, really big.

The cloud of gray began to clear. A figured towered before them. It coughed and spoke in a youthful, almost childlike giant's voice. "Where'd this smoke come from?" *Cough-cough!* "I don't see a fire!" The giant stood every bit of twenty feet tall. His build was strong and heavy. He had a small patch of messy blond hair on the top of his round head. One side of his face looked like it had been melted by fire, leaving the red rim around his eye gaping open. The other side of his face was clear and boyish. He peered down at Grey Cloak. "Why are your little ears pointed?"

"Uh... I'm Grey Cloak."

The giant caught a look at Breen. "Whoa, woman! Big little woman!" His gaze suddenly shifted toward the arachnamen. "Bugs! Barton hate bugs! Barton smash bugs!" The giant attacked. "Kill, kill, kill!"

Wide feet as long as a man was tall stomped three arachnamen at once. Bug guts squirted through the grass.

Barton scooped the arachnamen up and squished them in the palms of his hand. He grabbed a bigger one, bit its head off, and spit it out.

The arachna-queen reared back and screeched. She charged.

"Shut up!" Barton's fist hit her square in the face, breaking her teeth into shards.

The queen fastened onto Barton like a tick. Her pointed feet stuck into his body. Webs shot out of her mouth, and her fists beat him relentlessly.

"Attack!" Dyphestive cried. The Iron Sword swept through three arachnamen at once, splitting their torsos in two.

Breen grabbed two arachnamen by their necks and smashed their skulls together.

Grey Cloak slipped away from his attackers and went for the Rod of Weapons, which the queen had dropped. He kicked an arachnaman in the face, flipped over another, squirted between two more attackers, slid across the grass on his knees, and plucked the Rod of Weapons from the ground. "Got you!"

The rod's head flamed into a blade. He sliced a charging arachnaman's head off and gored another.

Barton and the queen fell toward Grey Cloak in a tangle of thrashing fists and limbs. He jumped out of the way. The ground quaked.

Thoom!

"Barton kill the giant spider! Barton hate the giant spider!" He headbutted the queen. "Spider ugly!" He fastened his grip around one of the queen's legs and ripped it off. "Take that, bug lady!" He beat her with it.

"Heads up!" Streak buzzed over the arachnamen. As they looked up, he filled their eyes with dragon flame. The bodies crackled and popped. The fire spread, eating their webbing up. Streak poured in more. "Burn, bugs! Burn!"

The queen pinned Barton underneath her, getting the best of him as she blew webs in his face.

"Dyphestive, back to plan A. Go for the big one!" Grey Cloak said.

"You don't have to tell me twice!" Dyphestive said. "Take the queen. Destroy the hive!" He skewered two arachnamen at once and flipped them over his shoulder.

Breen picked one up by its legs and flung it into the others. "Wait for me!"

Dyphestive arrived first. Muscular arms pumping, he cut off one of the queen's legs. Grey Cloak climbed on her back and started jabbing. He plunged the weapon deep and turned up the fire.

Barton ripped the webbing from his face and seized her neck. "Die, bug, die!"

The sea of arachnamen swarmed from all over, stabbing with their little spears and spitting bubbles of webbing. Chunks of bug guts splattered the company from head to toe.

The arachna-queen bucked out of Barton's grasp. Streak dropped out of the sky and set her head on fire. She screeched like a banshee and broke away from the summoned giant. Grey Cloak jumped off her back and landed on the ground. The arachna-queen limped away as fast as her remaining four legs could carry her. Her children followed, vanishing into the black veins inside the Rupture.

Barton shook his fist in the air. "And don't come back! Stoooopid bugs!" His huge body started to dissipate. He scratched his head. "Say, what's with all the smoke?" He started patting himself. "Go away. Go awaaaaaaaaaaaaaaaay..." His voice trailed off, and he vanished as quickly as he came.

34

DYPHESTIVE AND BREEN wiped the sticky webbing and arachnamen grit from each other's bodies. She was on one knee, and he stood facing her eye to eye.

"How many did you kill?" Dyphestive asked.

"I lost count after twelve." She picked off an antenna stuck to his cheek. "You?"

"I lost count after twenty. I think we could have taken all of them. Hold still." She had a spear stuck in her big thigh. He braced his boot against her leg and pulled it out. "Did that hurt?"

Breen shrugged her broad shoulders. "A little. Say, you're built for a little man."

"Thanks."

"Streak, get over here." Grey Cloak knelt beside Zanna's cocoon in a field of bug guts.

The runt dragon landed by Zanna.

"Give me some heat. I don't want to risk cutting her. This cocoon is tight."

"Sure thing." Streak breathed on the cocoon.

The strands started to separate and split apart. Using his hands, Grey Cloak ripped away the cocoon like he was peeling an orange. Zanna's fingers locked around his throat.

"Easy," he said in a raspy voice.

She let go of his neck and sat up. "That was awful." She rubbed her forehead with her palm. "I could breathe but only just."

"I didn't think it was so bad," Streak said. "At least from what I remember, it was like being in an egg again, but not as moist."

Grey Cloak offered his hand to Zanna and helped her up. "Are you able to stand?"

She closed her eyes and soaked in the sun. "This is much better." She gave him and the others a curious look. "You all look like you low-crawled through a field of rotten fruit." Her nose crinkled. "You smell like it too."

"You could say that," Grey Cloak said.

Zanna looked down at the giant foot impression on the ground. She met Breen's eyes. "That's not yours. Care to explain?"

"That's Barton's, a giant *boy*, I believe. I used the figurine to summon him. Speaking of which..." Grey Cloak made a quick search of the grounds and spotted the figurine. "Ah, there it is." He put it back inside his cloak. "Don't want to lose that. Apparently, we need it."

Streak sat on the ground and scratched behind his earhole. "You can say that again."

"Oh my." Zanna picked up a spiny black spider's leg that was twice as long as she was tall. "Is this from the thing that snagged me?"

They nodded.

She cast a worried look around. "And where is it?"

"It had enough of us and fled. Well, limped." Dyphestive flung gore off his sword. "Back to the Rupture."

"You should have finished it. I don't know where those things came from, but they didn't come from here." Zanna picked some cocoon out of her hair. "It was alien."

Breen spoke up, "They come from the pit, the Intersect."

"What are you talking about?" Grey Cloak asked.

The giant woman rose to her full height, making them look like children in her midst. She pointed at the Rupture. "That wasn't always there. It appeared no more than a decade ago, after the earth quaked. My people explored it and found a great hole in the world. Two of my brethren entered the black abyss, hoping to find ore in the earth. They did not return. My kind thought it best to fill it in or hide the spot. It appears the arachnamen dug it out and set up shop."

"How did they capture you?" Grey Cloak asked.

"Regardless of what the halflings say about us, we protect them. People from their villages blamed the giants. They said we feasted on them. You know how those rotten little acorns can spin a story." Her wooly eyebrows wiggled when she spoke. "Some people you can't help. Anyhow, I was told to explore the situation. I tracked the missing halflings back to the Rupture, as you coined it. I didn't make it far before I was trapped." She eyed Grey Cloak. "And I'd be dead, too, if you hadn't come around."

"Certainly, someone would have come for you," Dyphestive said.

"Not for weeks, at the soonest. We might look over the halflings, but they aren't a huge concern. Besides, I'm a giant. I should be able to take care of myself." She undid her braid, letting loose piles of lustrous red hair. She rustled it with her fingers. "I can't thank you all enough. If you need anything, well"—she pointed east—"we live that way, in the high hills. If any of my brood causes any trouble, tell them you're friends of Breen. They'll know what to do."

"We won't forget you," Dyphestive said.

Breen picked him up like a child and gave him a crushing hug. "You bet you won't, cutie!" She set him down and went after Grey Cloak. "Bring it in, rescuer?"

"I'm not a hugger."

She reeled him into her arms and hugged him tight.

Grey Cloak's back popped from the top of the spine to the bottom. It was like being squeezed by an anvil. As she set him down, his face was beet red.

Breen said, "We'll keep an eye on the arachnamen. Chances are, my people will want to finish them off." She gave a long wave goodbye and walked away, her arms swinging.

Grey Cloak looked between his brother and Zanna. "That was fun. Now what?"

35

DARK MOUNTAIN – THE PRESENT

A THUNDERSTORM RAGED over the jagged peaks that made up Dark Mountain. Bright flashes of lightning scattered across the sky, outlining the gray clouds. Cold rain came down in sheets. Waterdrops sizzled in the volcanic pits of lava.

With the wind tearing at his black-and-white robes, Gossamer followed Datris up the outer steps of the ziggurat. They were halfway up, and Datris moved with the ease of a cat in his woolen white robes. The younger elf's short brown hair didn't stir, but the pointed tips of his ears were as red as a rose.

Meanwhile, Gossamer's thighs burned like fire. Once a month, they checked in with Black Frost and were forced to make the agonizing journey from the bottom of the temple to the top. Thousands of slick steps switched back and forth, making the trek ever dangerous. Gossamer slipped more than a few times on the journey up.

Black Frost roared. His powerful lungs shook heaven and earth. Gossamer skidded on the slick steps. His knee hit the stone. Pain shot down his leg. He gritted his teeth.

Datris offered him a hand. "Let me help you."

"Thanks." Gossamer regained his footing. He wore sandals, and his toes were freezing. "Do your feet ever get used to this?"

Datris lifted his robes, revealing his blueish feet. "They get tougher, but it's always cold. It makes you appreciate the warmth."

Black Frost roared again. The temple trembled.

Gossamer clung to the walls. "What is he doing up there? It sounds like the world is going to end."

"He's feeding."

"Ah." Gossamer knew exactly what that meant.

Black Frost had been feeding on another world, Nalzambor, and growing in power. But from what Gossamer had seen, little of Nalzambor remained, and it was up to him to help save it. As they approached, he buried those thoughts. It was the only way he could survive.

Months ago, Gossamer had betrayed Grey Cloak and Dyphestive, sending them back in time using the Time Mural. It was a ruse to throw Black Frost off the heroes' trail. The dragon overlord had tasked his trusted servant,

Datris, with testing Gossamer's loyalty. Gossamer had failed the test. To his surprise, Datris had kept his secret. They'd been rebuilding the Time Mural that Gossamer had destroyed ever since.

The face-to-face meetings with Black Frost were terrifying. Gossamer never knew which one would be his last. He'd betrayed Black Frost more than once. He'd betrayed him from the very beginning, starting when Zanna Paydark, Grey Cloak, and Dyphestive were sent back in time. They'd filled him in. He'd been playing his part in a deceptive story ever since.

Gossamer paused as they neared the top.

"Are you well?" Datris asked.

"I want to catch my breath before we arrive."

"Yes, take a moment," Datris said politely.

Without Datris, Gossamer never would have made it so far. They said little to one another, knowing the less they knew, the better. They focused on Black Frost's tasks while silently working on the broader picture, saving Gapoli. Datris had been raised to be a Sky Rider, training secretly with twelve other brothers and sisters in Hidemark. Black Frost had singlehandedly destroyed them all, save Datris, who'd volunteered to serve him, just like Gossamer, by assisting Black Frost and betraying him at the same time.

"Are you ready?" Datris asked.

Gossamer nodded. His heart began to race. *How much longer can we fool Black Frost?* He buried his doubtful thoughts and refreshed them with others. *I am here to serve Black Frost. None other.*

They took the final flight of steps to the top of the temple and stood in sheets of icy rain and wind. Suddenly, Gossamer missed the shelter of the steps. He pulled his robes tight and tried to stop his teeth from chattering.

The temple platform glowed like warm sunlight underneath Black Frost's gargantuan form. They appeared little more than insects in his presence. For a moment, Gossamer forgot the cold rain soaking his limbs.

He's grown!

Black Frost's body filled the platform from one end to the other. His tail—like a great twisting oak tree—dangled over the far end of the platform.

With a body like that, he could swallow a grand dragon whole.

Dragons perched on the outer rim of the temple, facing outward. Grand dragons manned the corners, and middling dragons filled the space between. Ice and snow covered parts of their bodies, making them appear frozen like statues.

Datris took Gossamer's hand and towed him along. "Come."

Gossamer walked along Black Frost's body with a heart full of dread. Black Frost's shield-like scales were each nearly as big as the elf. Nothing in the world was large enough to fight him. Not one dragon, not one hundred.

How will we stop this monster?

They walked by Black Frost's front claw, which could scrape them away like insects, rounded the talon, and stood face-to-face with Black Frost. The dragon's eyelids—like curtains of steel—were closed. His warm breath produced steam, evaporating the rain and drying Gossamer's robes.

Black Frost spoke out of the corner of his mouth. "Tell me your progress."

Datris bowed. "Yes, mighty one. I'll let your faithful servant, Gossamer, speak on this."

Despite the warmth, Gossamer couldn't stop his teeth from chattering. "Yes, Lord Dragon, the Time Mural nears completion. I have all the resources I need, and the trials can begin soon."

"How soon?" Black Frost asked.

Gossamer swallowed. "After we return to the tower. Only a few more gemstones need to be configured. We should be able to open the Time Mural soon."

Black Frost opened one eye. "See that it is done. The world I feed on is at its end. I hunger for another. If you fail to find it, I'll feed on this world, starting with you two."

36

GOSSAMER AND DATRIS rode on horseback from Dark Mountain south toward the Wizard Watch in Ugrad. The freezing rain kept them company as well as a host of Black Guard riders. An escort always accompanied them from the towers. Inside the towers, more wizards in Black Frost's service kept track of when they came and went. Gossamer considered the long rides a blessing. It was the only place he and Datris could communicate privately.

Riding side by side with Datris, and well out of earshot of their host, Gossamer said, "It appears more is on the line than we originally anticipated."

"Agreed. I believe Black Frost has become addicted to his practice. I fear if we don't go back and stop him, our entire world will end."

"I know it's a lot to ask, Datris, but are you certain that when the time comes, you will change places with Zanna?"

Datris nodded. "I'll do it. I don't see a choice in the matter."

Gossamer had revealed to Datris that sometime in the future, he would switch places with Zanna and be turned into stone. At that point, Zanna would be sent back in time to find Grey Cloak and Dyphestive. Over the years, Gossamer had played everything out that Grey Cloak had described to him. Now he had to toe the line, but once a new portal opened, the future would be uncertain. They still had to find a way to kill Black Frost. And no one had an answer to that yet. In the meantime, they were borrowing time, literally.

The Wizard Watch in Ugrad stood in a forest of trees of dried and broken branches. No leaves colored trees. Instead, they were wrapped in black bark that rotted and fell away.

Birds crowed from nests in the high branches as the host of riders entered the dreary timberland. They rode toward the tower of stone in the center that stood taller than the surrounding trees. They arrived at the base of the watchtower an hour later, and every soldier looked up at the top of the great pillar. The structure was the same as all the others, with archways circling the tower, forming many levels. Most of the ancient building was covered in black moss and brown vines that snaked from the bottom to the top. At the base of the tower, the stones disappeared from one of the archways.

Gossamer and Datris dismounted, turned their horses over to the wide-eyed Black Guard, and entered the tower. The archway stones reappeared, sealing them inside. They stood in the main chamber with a great fountain in the middle, where water no longer flowed from the lips of the chiseled fish.

The towers of the Wizard Watch were marvels made by men and magic. A tower stood in every territory, all identical, all connected. A wizard could enter the tower in Ugrad and exit in Arrowwood. They were all the same but different.

Together, they entered a shaft that took them from the bottom level toward the top. They exited the shaft and approached the sealed doorway to the Time Mural's chamber, the same place where Gossamer and Grey Cloak had fought for their lives against the hydra. Claw marks from the epic battle scarred the walls.

Gossamer grimaced. He could still feel the wounds he'd suffered opening up again. And to think, he knew the fight was coming before it even came, and he fought it anyway. *Perhaps I'm mad.*

Datris gave him a concerned look. "Shall we continue?"

"Yes, of course." Gossamer plotted silently. They'd rebuilt most of the pedestal of power, but putting every last piece he'd destroyed back together again was a painstaking task. So long as they continued to work without interruption, they would finish the Time Mural soon. Getting it to work as Black Frost hoped was a more delicate matter. Even more so would be sending Zanna back in time. He passed his hand through the air. The archway rose. They entered and sealed themselves inside.

The Time Mural's archway stood intact with a stone wall behind it. A variety of large gemstones—emeralds, rubies, sapphires, topaz, and diamonds as big as a man's fist —were mounted in the archway in intricate runelike designs. It was a kingdom's-worth of precious jewels.

Facing the archway were two pewter thrones made out of solid metal. They were stout, square, and angular with hundreds of small divots in the arms from the underlings' fingernails. For a decade, Gossamer had suffered and labored, fulfilling their every cruel twist and whim. He'd borne it all for the greater good of the world.

Between the archway and thrones, off to the righthand side, the Pedestal of Power stood. The shattered plinth of rock had been meticulously rebuilt from the bottom up, like large pieces from a grand puzzle. At the pedestal's base sat piles of smaller gems the size of coins.

Gossamer picked up a handful of gemstones and joined Datris on the black marble foundation surrounding the pedestal. He stared into the small field of stones resting in the pedestal's base. Many of the spots needed to be filled in, and there were tens of thousands of combinations. He needed to configure one that worked.

Datris stood with his hands behind his back, looking down at the gems. "A daunting task. I don't envy you."

Gossamer added a sapphire and topaz into the mix. "Nor should you."

So far, everything had gone according to plan. Gossamer had even memorized some of the stones' configurations. But he hesitated. He wanted to make sure he could fully trust Datris. At that point, he couldn't turn back. Time was an issue with Black Frost so close to destroying one world and preparing to feast on another, their own.

With the coast clear, Gossamer decided to reveal his hand. "Datris, I need to tell you something."

The archway door opened. An imposing Risker in black armor strode into the room with his dragon helm tucked underneath his arm. A dark intent lurked in his eyes. His large hand gripped the pommel of his sword. A skinhead wizard stood beside him with a nasty scar down his cheek, burn marks on his face, and healed blisters and ugly tattoos on his arms. Many rings decorated his fingers.

Datris stepped down from the pedestal. "Who are you?"

The wizard spoke. "I am Honzur. This is Commander Covis."

"I respectfully ask you to leave. This is a private undertaking."

Honzur moved to the thrones and took a seat. Commander Covis joined him.

"We'll be staying," the wizard said. "We come and go as we wish."

"You have no authority here," Datris blustered. "You must leave. Black Frost—"

Honzur lifted a steady finger and returned a threatening gaze. "Black Frost is the one who sent us." He leaned back and smiled evilly. "We are here to observe and assist."

Gossamer was so close, and now he had two more obstacles to pass. His mind groaned. *Not now! No!*

37

LEAGUES NORTH OF DOVERUN, the burning wheels on Crane's wagon rolled to a stop on the sandy banks of the Great River. The fires on the wheels cooled, and Charro stomped the last flames from her hooves.

Crane set his horse whip aside and said in his jolly manner, "That was entertaining, wasn't it?"

Razor and Tinison spilled out of the back of the wagon first.

Tinison doubled over with his hands on his knees. "I think I'm seasick."

Zora exited the prisoner wagon next. She met Crane as he ambled out of the wagon and gave him a fierce hug. "It's so good to see you again!" She didn't let go, and he squeezed her back. "Thank you."

"The pleasure is all mine, as always." He spotted Gorva

wandering his way. "My betrothed, come greet your rescuer."

"No," Gorva said bluntly.

"Not even a hug?"

"One hug. A short one."

Crane ran into her arms, locked her up tight, and nuzzled her chest. "I've missed you, darling."

"We thought you were dead once. You don't want to be dead permanently, do you?" warned Gorva.

"No, of course not." Crane let her go and looked up into her heavy eyes. "I'd forgotten how gorgeous you were. As stunning as ever."

Gorva cracked a smile before walking away.

He nudged Zora with his elbow. "See, I'm wearing her down. Death does wonders for a man's reputation."

Shannon exited the wagon and gave Zora a firm handshake. "It's good to work with you again. I'm glad that worked out."

"Your father would be proud of you, Shannon." Zora noticed that the woman's ugly nose had mostly healed, revealing more of her strong, lovely features. "I wish he could have seen it."

"It's fine if you call me Beak. Actually, I prefer it. Adds character," Beak said.

"Beak it is," Zora said.

Tatiana approached. Her eyes grew when Crane rushed her.

"You might as well get it over with. He did save us after all." Zora gave a small grin.

"Ah, Tatiana." Crane embraced her. "Is Dalsay about? Or did he finally move on to, well, you know."

"Truth be told, I haven't seen him, but so far as I'm concerned, we're still together. Always."

"The next time I do a rescue, I hope it's a wagonload of unhitched women who love portly older men." He rubbed his belly. "Say, let's get something to eat. I know a great tavern north of here. Prettiest barmaids you've ever seen."

"Did someone say 'pretty, bar, and maid'?" Razor chimed in.

Tinison joined Razor at the hip. "Count me in." He ran a crude-looking comb through his wooly brown hair.

"We won't be making stops anytime soon. We need to run, or hide," Tatiana insisted. "It's only a matter of time before our enemies come after us. We have to get across the Green Riders and hide."

"If you ask me, none of this would have happened if Bowbreaker hadn't lost his mind," Razor said.

"It's not his fault. Queen Esmarelda already knew we were on the ship. They would have trapped us eventually." Zora craned her neck but saw no sign of Bowbreaker. "Where'd he go?"

"Where'd who go?" Razor asked.

"Bowbreaker."

Razor shrugged. "It wouldn't surprise me one bit if he went back to kill the queen. I say let him go."

Zora gave an aggravated sigh. "I'll go find him."

Gorva grabbed Zora by the elbow. "You should let him go. The ranger's way is not our way. He doesn't need a woman chasing after him."

"No, but he needs a friend." Zora jerked her elbow free and walked away, rubbing it. *Horseshoes, that woman is strong.*

She caught up with Bowbreaker at a small bend in the river. He stood toes-deep in the clear waters, looking across the expanse.

"Can we talk?"

"We have nothing to talk about. You're a strong woman, Zora. I'm honored to be among you and your friends, but I must finish what I started." He faced Zora and kissed her on the forehead. "I will not rest until Queen Esmarelda is dead."

38

ZORA RETURNED TO THE GROUP. "He left."

"Who left?" Tatiana asked.

"Bowbreaker. He's mad. Or maddening." Zora balled her fists. "He's actually going back after Queen Esmarelda. After all of this." She kicked the wagon wheel and screamed. "Ugh!"

"Easy now. I just had those detailed." Crane caught Zora's heated look and backed away. "It's already dirty anyway. Have at it."

Razor buckled on his sword belt. "Yeah, I'm really going to miss the conversation. Are we going somewhere to eat or no? I'm starving."

Zora exploded into a verbal tirade. "Of all the dirty things to do! That big-eared, pig-nosed, orc-faced ranger! I wouldn't let him shine the spit off my boots! A kiss on the forehead? Am I his child? His daughter? I should have kicked him in the nanoos! Busted him in the beans!" She yelled at the sky, "Auuuuuuuugh!"

Sergeant Tinison gave her a nod of approval. "Say, that was a good shout. Let it all out. But a little more from the abdomen."

Zora placed a dagger under his neck in the wink of an eye. "Perhaps you should go with Bowbreaker if you find me so amusing."

"I'm not amused." Tinison inched his face back. "I'm delighted. It's a compliment."

"Ugh!" Zora stuffed her blade back in her bandolier. She regarded everyone's concerned expressions. "What is everyone looking at? Haven't you ever seen a tantrum before?"

They all looked away. Crane averted his eyes and started whistling.

"I'm taking a walk." She pointed upriver. "That way. Don't anybody bother me!"

Without so much as a look over her shoulder, she made her way across the sandy bank of the river. On her way, she picked up a piece of driftwood and chucked it into the waters. She'd lost her head, but deep inside, it felt good. Bowbreaker's actions were inexcusable. Even Grey Cloak had never infuriated her so.

I don't deserve this. I deserve better. He's a fool. Arms crossed, head down, boots sinking in the packed sand, she continued her journey of self-exploration. *Why am I hung up on him? I barely know him.* Bowbreaker was as perfect an elf as she'd ever seen. He would be a perfect match for Queen Esmarelda. *Am I jealous? Of a woman he wants to kill? Maybe he really does care for her deeply. After all, I want to kill him.*

She climbed over a fallen log and headed closer to the water. She stepped on the edge of the bank and looked into her watery reflection. *No wonder he doesn't want me. I look like an urchin, like I used to be.* Deep down, another thought hurt more. *What if I never see him again? After all of this, why would I want to? But I do. Rogues of Rodden, I'm a mess.*

She turned toward the bank and jumped backward, stumbling into the river. She came up out of the water, unsheathing her dagger. "You!"

Anya stood on the bank suited up in dragon armor that shone in the sun. She wore her helmet, its wings flaring back on the sides. Blond-red hair spilled out from her helm over her shoulders. "You spook easily."

"You. Of all people." Zora climbed up the sandy bank but slipped.

Anya offered her a hand and pulled up.

"I'm soaking wet now." Zora flung the water off her fingers. "Perhaps I needed that."

"You were distracted and mumbling to yourself. Anyone could have crept up on you and slit your throat."

"Oh, thanks, Anya. I can always count on you to give it

to me straight." She rolled her eyes and pushed by the much taller woman. "And where have you been? Tatiana summoned you."

"I know. I'm here, aren't I?"

"A little late." Zora sat down on a beached log, took off her boots, and poured the water out of them. "Do you know what we've been through?"

"I know you and Bowbreaker are spatting."

Zora stuffed her feet back into her boots. "We aren't spatting. He has to be here to spat."

"I see. Well, don't spat with me because you have ranger problems. All this could have been avoided if we took the dragons north and not the slow river."

"We all agreed to divide forces. You said yourself traveling the skies would be dangerous. If we were spotted, our plans would have been undone." She didn't see any dragons in the area. "I take it you aren't alone? Or did you walk all this way?"

"Cinder is near."

"That's a great comfort. We were almost killed back in Doverun."

"I know. Cinder witnessed the event from the clouds. You slew three grands. Impressive. And you made it out, but the elves are coming, and they won't be alone. They'll send word to more Riskers. Now is as good a time to escape through the sky as any." Anya propped her boot on the log and took a small dagger from a hidden sheath. "They won't be looking up." She flipped the dagger. "They'll be looking down."

"What are we supposed to do, ride on Cinder's back? There are too many of us."

"It could be done. But first, we need to plan." Anya stuck the dagger back in the sheath. "So, if you're finished pouting, we need to join the others. We have more important matters to worry about."

"I'm not pouting."

"Good. Now tuck your lip back in and act like it. They need you, Zora. Now is not the time to lose your head over Bowbreaker."

With water squishing in her boots, Zora said, "Thanks for the kick in the pants, Anya."

"You're welcome."

39

"ARE you sure this is a good plan? I don't think it's a good plan," Crane said to Anya.

Talon hid behind the wood line overlooking the riverbank. The wagon was tilted onto its side, and Charro grazed nearby. "I mean, that's my wagon. If anything happens to it, I'll be beside myself with grief. That wagon's special."

"It will be fine. Calm yourself," Anya said.

Zora hunkered down in the cover of the ferns. She didn't much care for Anya's plan either. It seemed like a big risk to take, but Anya had convinced them that it wouldn't be difficult to outrun the elves and any dragons that pursued them. It was more important they throw them off the trail.

"Seriously, I don't want anything to happened to my

wagon, or Charro for that matter. Using them as bait is, well, cruel."

Anya clamped her hand over Crane's mouth. "Hush." She turned his head downriver. "They come."

A Risker came upriver riding a middling scout dragon. It glided several feet above the water, wings spread, leaving a wake from the wind. The dragon spotted the wagon and horse and squawked. It flew by, turned over the broad river, and doubled back. Its back claws skimmed the water, and it landed on the sandy bank.

Zora shrank down even farther.

The Risker's gaze scanned the wood line. The stout warrior climbed out of the saddle and drew his sword. He took a knee and put his hand on the footprints in the beach. His dragon sniffed the toppled wagon. He looked back into the woods and pointed. He spoke to his dragon but was too far away to hear. The dragon set its gaze on the woodland. It honked and snorted, then started walking toward the woods.

Cinder burst from the river. His immense jaws clamped down on the middling dragon's tail. He towed the smaller dragon toward the water. The middling dragon shrieked. Its front talons clawed up the bank, but it was no match for Cinder's great power. Cinder reeled the lesser dragon into the deep. They thrashed above and below the surface in a life-and-death struggle. Cinder dragged the dragon beneath the water's surface once and for all, never to be seen again.

By the time the Risker turned away from the slaughter in the waterway, Anya, Gorva, and Razor had him at the tips of their blades.

"Fools! You'll die for this!" He set his eyes on Anya. "You must be Anya! We were told the last Sky Rider died."

"You were told wrong," she said. "Drop your weapon."

"I'll die first!" The man spit. "Surrender, all of you! Submit before it's too late or die!"

"We aren't in a position to surrender, but you are," Razor said.

The Risker narrowed his eyes. "Listen to me, orc spit. I'll cut you to ribbons first."

Razor smacked the man's sword from his hand with the flat of his blade. He put the edge of his sword against the man's neck. "Will you now?"

Gorva took off the man's sword belt and patted him down. She removed a pair of small knives from his bracers and a slender dagger from his boot. She secured his hands behind his back. "You're very well prepared to wind up losing." She chucked his weapons into the river. "A shame you did."

"Fools! Every one of you. My brethren will come. They own the land! They rule the skies. It's only a matter of time before they catch up with you!" He sneered at them. "How much longer do you think you can survive. Huh? Days? Weeks? Hahahahaha! You won't last a month!"

Razor pulled out a coin. "He's a boastful one. Let's see who gets to kill him." He flipped the coin. "I call tails."

The coin landed on its side, buried in the sand.

"You can't even flip the coin properly," Gorva said. "I'll do it."

Anya grabbed the Risker by the collar and dragged him down toward the water. "I want to know how many Riskers are in pursuit. How many elves were sent?" She shook him. "Tell me."

"I won't tell you anything."

"Then you will die." Anya shoved him into the water.

"Anya, stop!" Zora said. "You can't kill the man in cold blood."

"Oh, but I can." She jerked the Risker up. "Do you want to die?"

"I don't care!" he said.

She shoved him back under.

"Are you out of your skull?" Zora asked. "Pull him up!"

"This man would feast on us all, and you want to save him?"

"I know he's scum, but we don't do it this way."

Anya lifted the man out of the water and shoved him aside. "Fine, you deal with him." She climbed out of the water and up the bank.

Gasping for air, the Risker spit water. "Your morals are

pathetic. They will be your downfall. It's only a matter of time before my comrades arrive and tear you apart piece by piece."

"You lie. A worm like you has no friends," Zora said.

"Ha, two more follow. Once they spot you, it'll all be over. They'll return to warn the others. And I'll be here all the while, smiling and laughing and taking a bath." He splashed water on his face. "Ah, refreshing."

Razor bristled. "Give the vermin a blade, and let me finish him."

Tatiana stepped forward. "I have a better idea."

"Oh-ho, I like to see what she thinks," the Risker said. "I'm Paltus." He winked. "At your service, beautiful thing."

"Bring him to me," she said.

"No need to manhandle me. I'll come right to you." Water dripped through his armor as Paltus marched up the bank. "Here I am, pretty elf. I can't wait to see your worst."

Tatiana stuck the Star of Light in his face. "Paltus, listen to me."

The man's eyes glazed over. His saggy chin quivered, and he said in a dreamy voice, "Yes, as you wish."

40

Paltus stood on the riverbank by the wagon, flagging down a pair of Riskers riding middlings.

Razor watched over Zora's shoulder, inside the wood line. "If this doesn't work, we're going to have to kill them all."

"Are you so eager to taste death?" Her palms sweat, and she took out her dragon charm. "But if this doesn't work, I'm ready."

"Yeah, well, I'm getting tired of setting up ambushes and not killing our enemies. It seems pointless to me."

"It's not an ambush. Now gum up so I can hear them and not you." She elbowed him and turned her attention to Tatiana.

Tatiana observed Paltus with an intense gaze. She held

the Star of Light in a white-knuckled grip. Her lips moved, but her words were silent.

The new arrivals landed and joined Paltus on the sand. Paltus's abrasive voice carried when he spoke, but Tatiana created his words. "I was ambushed by five dragons. They rescued the interlopers from my wrath and flew west toward Agustun. I overheard them discussing going to Monarch City. We must hurry and inform the elves if we're going to catch them!"

"Get on then!" One of the Risker's dark eyes swept over the grounds. He kicked his dragon. "To the skies!"

The Riskers took off. The dragons' wings beat the air, lifting them high toward the clouds until they looked like specks in the sky.

Crane stepped into the clearing first. Sweat glinted on his cheeks. "Whew! I can't believe that worked. What will happen when your spell wears off?"

Tatiana allowed herself a smile. "His mind will be goo, and he'll drool for several days, possibly longer."

"Perhaps you can use it on Razor," Gorva suggested.

"I've already got the drooling down, doll," Razor said. "As for my mind, it will always be as sharp as a razor."

"Someone help me tilt the wagon back over. We still have a long journey ahead," Crane said.

Gorva, Razor, and Tinison gathered at the wagon. Before the men could place their hands on it, Gorva shoved it over. She dusted off her hands and walked away with a smile, leaving the men gaping.

Tinison combed his hair. "I think I'm in love. What did you say her name was?"

"Gorva. And she loves flowers. Tulips are her favorite. And be aggressive. She's an orc. They like that," Razor suggested.

"Understood." Tinison hurried after Gorva.

Crane joined Razor. "You're going to get him killed. You know that, don't you?"

"Aye." Razor elbowed Crane. "But that's less competition for us." His gaze met Beak's. "Excuse me. I see someone I need to fully acquaint myself with."

Crane hitched Charro back to the wagon. "All right, everyone, load up. We have a long way to go and a short spell to get there."

"You have a place in mind?" Zora asked.

"I told you I did. Just inside the Green Ridges. I have family there, Jerry and Reed." Crane climbed into the wagon. "They'll take care of us."

Anya walked down the bank with her helmet under her arm. Her lustrous, long hair flowed down past her shoulders. "We'll keep a lookout from the sky."

Cinder emerged from the river, making everyone jump and draw their weapons. Water cascaded down his scales as he moseyed out of the river. He shook like a dog, showering everyone.

"Cinder!" Anya said.

"Heh-heh." He lowered himself to the ground. "You'll dry quickly after we take off. No worries," the grand dragon said in a fatherly manner.

Anya put on her helmet and climbed on. "Ride the Sky!"

Cinder spread his wings and pounded the air like a sudden storm.

Zora turned her face and held onto the wagon.

Anya the Sky Rider took flight and soon vanished from sight.

"Are you coming?" Beak asked Zora.

"Oh, sure." She climbed onto the front bench and sat between Crane and Beak. She glanced back at the others, who'd piled into the back of the open wagon. She'd almost forgotten about Bowbreaker until she saw Razor spinning one of his arrows between his fingers. She turned around and faced front. "Let's go."

"As you wish," Crane said. "Charro, *giddyap*."

Green Ridge was a leagues-long mountain range that created a natural divide between Arrowwood and Ugrad. The spectacular hills stretched out from the Outer Ring and beyond Farstick. The air was crisp and clean. The tree leaves in the expansive hills were all different shades of green. High grasses with fields of limestone jutting out covered many of the boundless hills. Sheep and cattle roamed the hills, guarded by shepherds wearing colorful robes and carrying large, hooked staffs.

The wagon rumbled by. Crane waved at the men in the fields, who didn't so much as return a nod.

"It's a beautiful place, but I'm not sure we're welcome here." Beak leaned forward and looked at Crane. "Are you sure we're welcome?"

"Of course. I know people," he said.

"You said the same thing in Salt Knob. As I recall, they ran us off."

"That was a simple misunderstanding. Trust me. Jerry and Reed are like family."

"I thought you said they were family," Zora said.

Crane shrugged absentmindedly. "Family. Friend. It's all the same to me."

"Uh-huh," Zora and Beak replied.

Razor cozied up behind the women sitting on the bench. "Are we there yet? My back and buttocks are killing me."

"Don't ask us. Ask him," Zora said.

"Crane, tell me we are close," Razor demanded.

"Only a few more leagues." He pointed at the highest crest among the green hills. "We're going there."

Razor squinted. "That's not leagues away. That's a day, if not two."

"Ah, quit whining." Crane grinned. "It'll be worth it when we get there. I promise."

41

"It's breathtaking, isn't it?" Crane asked.

"I've never seen the likes of it," Zora replied.

They'd arrived at the lodge in the hills a few hours earlier. The lone roadway had been a relatively steep climb that wound around the mountain and seemed to take forever to get to the top. The lodge was made from ancient timbers built into the rocky cliffs overlooking a spectacular view of the surrounding valleys. Everyone settled into their rooms and met at the tavern on the deck. The company sat outside at a long table with bench seats and dug into their food. The mountains were chilly, but a stone fireplace on the end of the deck provided ample warmth.

A waterfall spewed from the rocks below the massive wooden girders that held up the decks and the lodge. It fed a crystal-clear lake below. Bearded antelope drank from the cold waters. A pair of black bears romped in the waterfall's base.

"How's the view?" a bony man asked in a strong, obnoxious, yet charming voice. He slapped his strong hands on Crane and Zora's shoulders and craned his long neck over the porch. "Look at those antelope. That's good eating! Hold on a moment." He turned around and cupped his hands around his mouth. "Jerry! Get the crossbow. Send Fred down to the lake! The antelope are feeding! And tell Fred no swimming. No one up here wants to see his hairy behind."

"You're going to kill them?" Zora asked. "But they're so beautiful."

"If you think they're beautiful now, wait until you taste them." He kissed his fingers. "Simply divine! Oh, pardon my manners. I don't believe I've introduced myself." He wiped his hands on his greasy white apron. "I'm Reed, and you are?"

"Zora."

"Lovely, lovely name." He kissed her hand. "And face too. So, how did you get tangled up with this old hound dog?"

Zora shrugged. "Fate, I guess."

"Yeah, fate. That was the only reason I ran with him, and it didn't take long before I ran away and bought this place. Been hiding from him ever since." Reed spread his arms wide. "Yet here I am! He found me!"

Crane chuckled delightedly. "You should know as well as anybody that you can't hide from me. I'm like a bad chip. I keep turning up."

"You can say that again." Reed patted Crane's belly. "So, *brother*, who are you running from this time?"

"Me? Running?" Crane gave an innocent look. "Whatever do you mean?"

Reed turned and pointed at the long table hosting the rest of Talon. "I'm talking about that. Those aren't typical sightseers. Look at them."

Everyone feasted on stacks of hot food, grasping their meal with dirty fingers.

"They look like death spit them up." He waved his hand in front of his nose. "And they stink too. That's why I had to separate you from the other guests. I didn't want to spook them. People are jumpy these days. That's why they come here, to relax."

Leaning with his elbows on the railing, Crane locked his fingers. "It's been a long journey. What do you expect?"

"I'll tell you what I expect. I expect no trouble. We've worked awfully hard to keep this place hidden from you-know-who. That's why people come here. I'll put you up for the night, but you need to move on tomorrow." Reed dropped his hand on Crane's shoulder. "That's the best I can do, old friend."

Crane nodded. "Your hospitality is more than generous, as always, brother. We'll be gone by first light."

"Good. Now that we have business out of the way, I'll turn up the hospitality." Reed clapped his hands. "Girls. Bring out the good mess." He moseyed behind the table, touching everyone's shoulders and pointing at the food. "Try this. Try that. Do you need more rolls? Girls! More rolls! These lads are hungry!"

"Interesting company you keep. He's very *accommodating*," Zora commented.

"We can trust Reed and Jerry. I wouldn't have brought you here if we couldn't." Crane looked outward at the burning sun settling behind the hills. "Once this is over, perhaps we can all come back and stay a while."

"Perhaps." Zora's stomach moaned. "I'm starving. Shall we eat?"

"I thought you'd never ask."

They joined the others at the table and ate. Everyone enjoyed themselves and ate heartily. Razor sawed off a hunk of ham and practically swallowed it in one gulp. Tatiana giggled at Crane's jokes, hiding her smile behind a goblet of wine. Even Gorva showed a toothy grin and soaked in Razor's boasts. Talon was family, one and all—imperfect in many ways but perfect in others. Despite their differences, they fought with one another and for one another, willing to give their lives to save the world. They were a few good people, attempting the ridiculous, hoping to achieve the impossible.

Zora drank deeply. The sweet wine warmed her lips.

She eased back in her chair, let Reed put a blanket over her lap as the sun went down, and allowed herself to enjoy one after another of Crane's stories. The feast went on for hours. They enjoyed music, dancing, and Reed and Jerry plucking away at the strings.

"It's a shame every day can't be like this," she said to Crane.

"If it were, you wouldn't appreciate it so much. Peace isn't something you keep if you don't work hard for it." He polished off another goblet of wine, turned his head away, and burped. "Excuse me. That went down too fast."

"Zora!" Razor hollered from the opposite end of the table. "How long are we staying? This place is fantastic!"

She and Crane exchanged an plucky look.

"Don't worry about it!" she said over the music. "We'll talk about it tomorrow."

Crane beamed. "Good answer."

42

THE PAST

STRIPPED DOWN TO HIS TROUSERS, Grey Cloak waded into a cove on the edge of the Great River. He rinsed the blood off his face then drenched his shirt in the water and wrung it out. He had bruises up and down his arms and on his chest. His face was swollen. Squeezing the mud between his toes, he submerged himself in the river then came back up and flung his hair back out of his eyes. "Ah!"

Zanna had been training him and Dyphestive for months. Her sessions often involved the blood brothers sparring with one another by trying to beat each other's skulls in. Hitting Dyphestive was like hitting a bag of sand, but he still probed for a weakness. He used his superior speed to outmaneuver his brother, but Dyphestive had gotten much better at anticipating his moves. A well-placed punch had flattened Grey Cloak. Zanna had stopped the training after that.

He wiped his eyes and wrung out his hair. "Ten years of this." He sighed. "I'm not doing ten years."

He and his mother, Zanna, had gone back and forth about many disagreements. She continued to insist they lie low, and she made a strong point after their last encounter at the Rupture that had almost killed them. Every day, she tried to persuade them to return to the tower. Every time, they refused.

Grey Cloak had a theory. Zanna wanted to make life so miserable on the outside that they would want to go inside. He saw through it and wouldn't give in.

"The cold belly of a flinty tower is no place for an elf," he told her time and again.

Dyphestive agreed.

So, in the meantime, while they weren't training, they set snares and traps for game, picked berries, gathered firewood, and worked on building their tiny cabin in the woods, which gave them shelter from the rain.

Zanna the taskmaster made Rhonna the dwarf's efforts look rudimentary. Grey Cloak didn't understand why they listened to her at all, other than the fact that she was his mother. He would have questioned the validity more if their resemblance weren't so strong. And to make matters worse, Dyphestive liked her.

He slipped through the water into a shallow spot in the

cove with a bank of river rocks. He sank back into a nook that kept him hidden from the forest. "Perfect."

The Great River sat off in the distance. Its swift waters ran south, and not a single boat passed by. Legend had it that at the end of the river, a great waterfall dropped off the edge of the world and fed another. Like he considered most legends, Grey Cloak found it ludicrous. The river could flow wherever it wanted to, and he could care less where it went. He only wanted to go to a place that had people in it.

He closed his eyes and enjoyed the sound of water slapping against the rocks and a bird's song. His breathing slowed. The soreness in his throbbing muscles eased. He let himself relax.

"Excuse me," a little voice said.

Grey Cloak peeked open an eye.

A halfling woman in a blue dress sat on the edge of the surrounding rocks. She had a cute face, freckles, a button nose, and pile of brown hair twisted around her head like the cap of an acorn.

He pushed up out of the water. "Can I help?"

"You might not remember me, but I am Keena." She kicked her bare, little feet as she spoke. "You rescued me from the spiders. I've never been so terrified before. I wanted to thank you."

"Oh, well, you're welcome, Keena. I'm glad I could help."

"I wanted to thank you too!" A second halfling

appeared behind Keena. He had curly brown hair and wore a long-sleeved cotton jerkin and trousers. The Cloak of Legends covered his shoulders. "I'm Bosco the Mender. I can stitch anything. This ratty cloak, for instance. I can sew in some style." He shrugged his eyebrows in an enticing manner. "The ladies like fancy designs." He tugged on Keena's sleeve. "Look at the white stitching on my wife's sleeves. They're daisies. Aren't they beautiful?"

"Give me back that cloak," Grey Cloak warned. "It's mine!"

They cowered behind the rocks. From their cover, Bosco tossed the cloak away. It fell into the water. "Don't slay us! We meant no offense! We come to pay respect!"

"And ask for help," Keena said.

"Shhhh. He's mad enough. We don't want to spring that on him yet. He saved us once. I told you about this."

The couple bickered back and forth.

Grey Cloak could hear every word but couldn't understand their quick-tongued halfling speak. He hauled his cloak up out of the water and slapped it down on the rocks. Leaning over the rocks, he stared down at the halflings. "Sorry I scared you, but I'm very attached to my cloak."

The halflings bounced to their feet.

"So you'll help us?" Bosco asked.

Keena slapped her hand over his mouth and whispered in his ear, "We didn't even tell him what we wanted. Let me handle this, will you?"

Bosco nodded.

Grey Cloak made himself comfortable on the rocks, perhaps out of pure boredom. The halflings piqued his curiosity. "I'm interested in what you have to say. Let's hear it."

Their jaws opened, but neither spoke.

"Go ahead. Somebody say something. Out with it."

Bosco poked Keena. "Tell him. Tell him."

"Oh, yes," she said. "Someone stole a precious idol of ours."

"Among other things," Bosco added.

"Hush, Bosco," Keena replied. "Grey Cloak, we need you to retrieve it."

43

Grey Cloak led Keena and Bosco back to his camp.

Zanna's eyes turned stormy the moment she saw the halflings. She was quick to pull Grey Cloak aside. "May I have a word with you?"

"Certainly. Dyphestive and Streak, acquaint yourselves with Keena and Bosco," he said.

Dyphestive carried a log on his shoulder, and he dropped it to the ground. "Will do."

Streak scurried across the ground and sniffed the cowering halflings with the tip of his tongue. "Don't worry, halflings. I won't eat you unless you want me to. The name is Streak, and you are?"

Zanna dragged Grey Cloak behind their cabin. "What do you think you're doing, leading strangers to our dwelling?"

"They're part of the group we saved from the Rupture, perfectly harmless."

"Is that so? Because I don't remember seeing them, do you?"

"Er... well, no, but as I recall, you were in a cocoon most of the time. Besides"—he shrugged—"they seem like honest people."

"Don't be a fool. Halflings are excellent spies." Zanna peeked around the corner. "Not to mention thieves. They'd pluck out your eyeballs while you slept if they thought they were worth something."

"Them?" Grey Cloak took a gander at the halflings. One was riding on Streak's back, and the other sat on Dyphestive's shoulders. "I don't see it. Look, I don't think it will do any harm to hear them out. They'll go away."

Zanna tilted her head. "Hear them out? What are you talking about?"

"They said their idol was stolen. They want us to take it back." He smirked. "See? Harmless."

"You didn't commit to that, did you?"

"Of course not."

"You need to get rid of them. Tell them to go away."

"Come now, Zanna. Have a heart. They're scared. Besides, a little adventure on the side will be good for us."

Zanna stiffened. "Need I remind you that the trip to the Rupture almost got us killed?"

"Hmmm." Grey Cloak tapped his chin, appearing to be

in deep thought. "Come to think of it, you haven't reminded me of that since, oh, the *last time I saw you*."

"Don't be a smart mouth." She turned him around and shoved him from behind the cabin. "Get rid of them."

"You know their kind. They don't like to take no for an answer."

"They'll leave if you threaten them. Now go."

"Zooks. What do you have against helping halflings?" He wandered away to the others.

With Keena on his shoulders, Dyphestive rushed up to Grey Cloak. "We have to help them."

Streak carried Bosco on his back. "Absolutely. They need our help, or they'll starve to death."

"I see." Grey Cloak turned around, faced Zanna, and smirked. "That's three votes to help them to your one."

Bosco and Keena raised their little hands.

"Correction, that's five votes to one, Lady Zanna," Bosco said.

Zanna's gaze could have burned a hole through them all.

"She carries an awful scowl," Keena whispered. "Does she always look so mean?"

"I hate to tell you, Keena," Grey Cloak said as he walked away, "but that's her smile."

"Tell us more about your idol, Bosco," Grey Cloak said.

They'd begun the trek northeast through the forest, and he carried the little man on his shoulders while Dyphestive still carried Keena.

"Is it big?"

"It's magical. It brings us good harvests and keeps our families safe." Bosco ducked under a tree branch. "I always wanted to be tall, but I can see the disadvantages. You will see when we find it. It's a gorgeous stone shaped like a dragon. It's been in our possession for centuries. We're doomed without it."

Grey Cloak looked back at Zanna, whose frown was as long as a river.

"See, Zanna? They would be doomed without it."

Zanna walked with her arms crossed. "If it protects them, then how did it get stolen? Don't be fooled by this pair. They probably worship a river rock they dredged up months ago. They're very superstitious people."

"It's not a rock," Keena fired back. "It's a magic idol. You'll see."

"Oh, I can't wait," Zanna said.

Grey Cloak didn't care what it was. He'd gotten so bored in their camp that he would do anything. A short journey would give his morale a boost. Even Dyphestive and Streak had become bored with the isolation and training. They needed some excitement, even if it came in the form of appeasing a pair of goofy halflings. Besides, the little people weren't such bad company. They were very friendly.

"I'm curious," Zanna continued, "if you know where the idol is, why haven't you tried stealing it back yourselves? I for one know how *resourceful* halflings can be."

Bosco vigorously shook his head. "Oh no, we would never venture into the Temple Ruins. It's far too dangerous."

"The Temple Ruins, you say?" Zanna sounded concerned. "Oh, that's brilliant. Well played, Grey Cloak."

"Is that a problem?" He caught Dyphestive's curious look.

"Didn't you pay any attention at Hidemark? Don't you remember the lessons about lore?" Zanna asked.

Grey Cloak replied, "Well, I—"

"In my defense, I never had the privilege." Dyphestive ducked so Keena wouldn't bump her head on the branches. "What's significant about temple ruins? We've come across them before."

"These are no commonplace temple ruins your little friend speaks of. It is *the* Temple Ruins, a fallen civilization ruined by greed and cursed by evil, a place whose real name is never spoken." Zanna's tone was deadly serious. "Where bold treasure hunters enter and never return."

Bosco jabbed his stubby finger in the air and said excitedly, "Yes! That's the place!"

44

THE FOREST SHIFTED into a more junglelike terrain. Broad deep-green leaves covered the gnarled branches of the monster trees. The trees' roots were exposed in most places, where the bright eyes of frightened critters huddled in the dark shelters.

Cawing birds spoke in the high branches, making sounds Grey Cloak had never heard. The heat became suffocating, and his clothing clung to his body.

"How far is this place?" he asked.

"Not far." Bosco wrung sweat from his handkerchief. "Keep walking this way."

Dyphestive smashed a mosquito bigger than his hand. He wiped it onto the bark of a tree. "Is this still Gapoli?"

Zanna cut through vines blocking their path with her

sword. She swept the sweat from her brow as Grey Cloak passed. "This idol better be magic."

"It is. You'll see." Keena drank from a waterskin. "We'll need more water soon." She held it up to her mouth and squeezed out the last drops. "Very soon."

"I hear the Temple Ruins have beautiful thirst-quenching fountains this time of year," Zanna said.

"They do?" Bosco smacked his lips. "That sounds fabulous."

"Don't listen to her, Bosco. She makes jokes that are hard to understand because they aren't any good."

"Ah, sarcasm. We like sarcasm," Bosco replied. "My ears are bigger than my feet. Hah-hah!"

Grey Cloak stopped and spread his arms. "No one move." A giant albino white-and-yellow python slowly slithered across his path. Its body stood higher than Grey Cloak's knees. "That's one big snake."

Bosco locked his arms around Grey Cloak's head, covering his eyes. "Save me! Save me!"

"It won't attack us unless we attack it." Grey Cloak peeled the halfling's arms away. "See? It's almost gone."

Bosco panted for breath. "Puff-puff-puff-puff..."

Grey Cloak said, "Who stole the idol to begin with?"

"Now you ask?" Zanna said.

"It was the Red Backs," Keena said quickly. "We didn't see them, but we followed their footprints here. They're trouble."

"Yeah, nothing but trouble." Bosco sneered. "They come around every season, bartering their shells for our grain. We keep an eye out for when they come, but the last time, they caught us in the autumn celebration, when our idol is on full display. They stole it, yes, they did. Rampaged our vault in the dark of night and stole it away." He spit. "Pah-too! I hope you kill them all."

"What's a Red Back?" Dyphestive asked.

"A race of lizardmen," Grey Cloak said. "See? I paid attention during some of the lore sessions."

"They aren't a race of lizardmen but a tribe of wicked lizardmen who tend to be the henchmen to an even darker and more vile master," finished Zanna.

"I could have told you that," he said.

Keena tousled Dyphestive's hair. "Don't worry, mighty warrior. You destroyed the spiders. You can destroy them."

"Well, to be truthful, we didn't kill the arachna-queen," Dyphestive admitted. "She ran away."

"Oh, that's bad. If you don't kill the beast, it will come back to haunt you," Bosco said.

"Why didn't you ask the giants to help?" Grey Cloak asked.

"Giants. *Blecht!* We hate giants. They eat our people. Don't believe a word they say," replied Bosco.

"Have you ever seen a giant eat a halfling?" Zanna asked.

"Yes, dozens of times," Bosco admitted.

"No, we haven't." Keena braided the top hairs on Dyphestive's head. "But that tale has been going around for centuries."

"Shush, Keena!" Bosco said.

"Don't shush me. You shush!"

"You're my wife. If I say shush, you shush."

"I'll remember that the next time you want me to bake you a blackberry pie," she said.

Bosco lurched. "No shushing then, but we don't like the giants. We hate them. They ate us before. They'll eat us again. That's what I say. Oh, the day will come." He raised his tiny voice. "And we will all be shushed forever!"

The company trudged along the marked paths they could find and plowed through the thicker foliage. The longer they walked, the hotter it became. Butterflies the size of a man's head floated by, and ugly toads as big as hounds snatched them out of the air with extraordinary tongues.

Grey Cloak was sticky from head to toe by the time they stopped in front of a wall of ferns that stood twice as tall as them.

"This is it," Bosco whispered in his ear. "The Temple Ruins' entrance."

"I better take a look for myself." He reached up to grab Bosco, but the halfling jumped down.

"Good luck to you!" Bosco slapped Grey Cloak on the behind. With his arm over Keena's shoulder, he waved.

"We'll wait here for you, but try to make it quick. Good food is scarce in these parts, and I'm famished. It will be dark soon, but we'll be fine."

"Streak, are you still in there?" Grey Cloak asked.

The runt dragon popped his head out of Grey Cloak's hood. "I'm ready. Let's do this."

Dyphestive and Zanna lined up beside Grey Cloak.

"Are you sure you want to go through with this?" Zanna asked.

"Anything has to be better than training with you." Grey Cloak took his time and pushed through the long row of ferns. "What is this, a cornfield?" He swam through it step-by-step, made it to the other side, and faced a sunken valley consisting of fields of fallen stone structures.

Dyphestive popped out beside him. "The Temple Ruins, huh? Fitting."

45

WITH GREY CLOAK leading the way, the trio crept down a bank thick with ivy into the sunken valley. The Temple Ruins were a field of great stones and rock structures that appeared to have been abandoned ages ago. Towering pylons broken into several pieces lay fallen across the grassy landscape. Pyramids of varying sizes sat scattered across the dewy grasses of the valley. The ancient buildings had many levels and appeared to be homes or possibly storehouses.

"Their idol could be anywhere." Zanna sidled by Grey Cloak. "There are dozens of these things."

"I'm sure we'll find a way to narrow it down," he said.

Dyphestive tapped his brother on the shoulder and pointed at the ground. "Prints."

Grey Cloak noticed the heavy impression of a Red Back

lizardman's footprint. "See? The Red Backs will lead us right to the idol. I promise."

"Perhaps, but don't be overconfident. The Red Backs aren't the servants of ordinary beings," Zanna said.

"You never know. They might be out for themselves." With darkness falling, Grey Cloak stole through the ruins. His keen eyes followed a faint path in the grass.

Traffic had picked up in the area, and the lizardmen footprints became more frequent. Streak poked Grey Cloak's ear with his snout. Grey Cloak stopped in his tracks and followed the dragon's nose turned toward the sky. A Red Back sat on top of a ten-foot-tall structure. The lizardman blended in with the stones, and the shadows blacked out most of his muscular body. Grey Cloak pointed out the lizardmen to the others. They moved on and stole their way inside one of the smaller abandoned buildings.

"Well, we have proof of lizardmen," he said. "We'll have to be more careful from here on out. Keep your eyes peeled, and stay close to me."

They exited through the other side of the entrance and scoped out the surrounding structures before they moved. The burly silhouettes of the Red Backs stood among the structures, and a few of them patrolled on foot. Using the cover of darkness, the group darted from one structure to the other, moving deeper into the valley.

Grey Cloak's nose twitched. He smelled smoke and cooking meat. He led them along the base of another structure, rounded the corner, and stopped in full view of a large stone temple that dwarfed the others, which stood several stories tall.

Red Back lizardmen clustered together, standing around a huge bonfire. A large beast roasted on a spit at the base of the temple.

"Smells good," Dyphestive said under his breath.

"We didn't come for dinner." Grey Cloak noticed a stone staircase that led to an entrance to the temple at the top. "The idol must be in there. I'll take a look."

"Oh no, you don't." Zanna grabbed his arm and pulled him back. "I warned you about the Temple Ruins. They're a death trap. If you go in there, you won't come out."

"Does it really look that dangerous to you?"

"No, but looks can be deceiving. We need to wait and see what comes in and out. The Red Backs are clearly serving something. That's why they're preparing a ceremonial feast." Zanna squeezed his elbow. "Be patient."

"Easy. I can wait it out." Grey Cloak leaned back against the wall. "I'm only rushing for the halflings' sake. They're probably hiding in a tree, terrified. You know, when daylight comes we'll be exposed."

"Well, that won't be for a while." Zanna turned to Dyphestive. "Have you ever been able to talk any sense into your brother?"

"You have to catch him at the right time," Dyphestive said.

Grey Cloak didn't wait to hear the rest of the conversation. He lifted the Scarf of Shadows over his nose and headed toward the temple.

"Uh, Zanna, I hate to tell you this." Dyphestive looked over her shoulder. "But..."

She whipped her head around. Grey Cloak and Streak were gone. "That crazy little fox. I should have known better than to turn my back on him."

"The temple doesn't look that dangerous, in my humble opinion. The Red Backs look more fearsome than it."

Zanna smirked. "Perhaps it isn't. Perhaps it is."

Dyphestive gave her a curious look. "Ah, I see. You don't want him messing with any of this, do you? So you told him a lie?"

"No, I tried to spook some sense into him. Like I said, halflings are superstitious people. This idol could be anything. It's not worth risking our lives over. They'll forget about it soon enough and create another idol." She shook her head. "But your brother doesn't want to keep his head down. He wants action. Well, let him have it. If he needs us, we'll be waiting."

Dyphestive grunted. "I suppose it's a good exercise." He stared at the temple. The full moon cast a haunting light on the rocks. "Do the Red Backs really serve something, or was that made up too?"

Zanna slipped a dagger from the sheath on her thigh. "No, they're henchmen, as I said. But they're dumb brutes, who serve anything that can dupe them. No doubt something inside that temple has caught their attention or manipulated their minds." She flipped the dagger into the ground. "We'll have to wait and see until Grey Cloak finds out."

"You don't seem too worried."

She shrugged. "He's a well-armed natural. I think he'll be able to handle this. But as I said, we'll be here to bail him out."

Dyphestive stuck his sword point-first into the ground. He focused on the temple and the lizardmen. "Good, but I'm not going to wait here too long."

46

THE RED BACK lizardmen stood by the fire, talking in low, gruff voices while one of them turned the large spit's handle. Unlike most lizardmen Grey Cloak had encountered, the Red Backs' skins were a mud-red color, and spiny red ridges of hair ran from their necks to the tips of their tails. Thick yellow claws adorned their hands and feet, and each of them moved like a stocky juggernaut.

Grey Cloak had no trouble slipping by them. Cloaked in invisibility, he moved to the bottom steps of the temple and began his ascent. The temple was far bigger than it appeared from a distance. The wide steps were as tall as two normal ones. Halfway up the staircase, a tunnel entrance opened, and he entered.

"*Entrez vous*," Streak said.

The temple was pitch-black inside. Grey Cloak lowered the Scarf of Shadows and turned on the Rod of Weapons's light. The tunnel was clear, the stone walls smooth, and moonlight poured in from the exit on the other side.

"Interesting."

The temple wasn't unique. The walls weren't covered with ancient pictography, runes, and symbols, just the grainy texture of stones that had been chiseled ages ago. The ceiling, a black tapestry of rock, looked as smooth as glass.

Streak saw his reflection in the ceiling. "Pretty."

Halfway through the temple, Grey Cloak came to a four-way intersection revealing three more tunnels like the one he'd entered. "Isn't this delightful? One temple, four tunnels, and nothing else."

"Maybe you missed something," Streak commented.

"I didn't see any other doorways. Did you?"

"Nope."

He looked down. "Say, this is unique."

A huge painted sunburst decorated the smooth marble floor. Tiny images of people walking on the flames appeared to tell a story. Grey Cloak traced the train of people that were little more than stick figures acting out a scene from everyday life.

"It looks like they're feeding a man into a pit *heeeeeeeer—*"

The floor dropped out from under Grey Cloak's feet, plunging him into darkness. Hungry flames waited to devour him below. The Cloak of Legends blossomed out. He floated toward the churning fire ever so slowly.

"Streak, get us out of here!" he said.

The runt dragon crawled out of his hood. "Grab onto my tail!"

Grey Cloak latched onto Streak's tail. The dragon pumped his wings, and they started to rise.

Piece by piece, the floor they'd dropped through started to magically fill in.

"Faster, Streak, faster!"

"I'm going as fast as I can." Streak grunted. "Have you gained weight?"

"I don't know." Grey Cloak frog-kicked his legs. "Faster!"

"That's not helping." Streak flew through the closing gap.

Grey Cloak tucked his feet into his chest.

The floor sealed closed beneath him. He let go of Streak's tail and scrambled out of the intersection.

Streak landed beside him. "Close call, eh?"

Grey Cloak caught his breath. "It's a good thing we came alone. Anyone else would have been finished." The sunburst pattern on the floor glowed a fiery orange and cooled back to black.

"Now I know why no one who comes ever leaves. Zanna

was right," Grey Cloak admitted. "Dark magic is afoot here."

"Perhaps we should leave. Tell the halflings you found them another idol. You'll think of something," Streak suggested.

"I think you might be right." Grey Cloak heard stone grinding on stone. He turned and peered down the long tunnel to the exit. A slab of rock at the end of the tunnel sealed them in. "It appears that we aren't going anywhere."

Streak flicked his tongue. "I have a bad feeling about this."

"Yeah, so do I." Grey Cloak stood. He hadn't dealt with many traps before. Battling flesh and blood was one matter. Fighting against the crafty mind of the unseen was another. "Don't fret. I'll think of something."

"You better, because you can't expect me to bail us out every time. I'm pretty young, you know."

Grey Cloak headed down the tunnel one step at a time, poking the walls, ceiling, and floor with the Rod of Weapons the entire way. The solid walls held only the smallest seams. He saw no signs of a door, hatch, or anything remotely helpful. After a painstaking search, he made it to the opposite end, where the stone slab blocked their exit.

"We have to find some way to open this."

"Try knocking." Streak pecked at it with his snout. "Ow,

that might not work. Perhaps it needs a secret word. I'll try one. *Open sesame*."

"Where did you come up with that?"

"Alter-Earth."

"Never heard of it. Stand back." Grey Cloak summoned wizard fire into the Rod of Weapons, forming the burning end of a spear. He jammed it into the rock and fed his power into it. His brows knitted together. The spot radiated like a bright keyhole. He fed more power into the rock. "It's thick!"

"I can see that."

Grey Cloak pulled the rod out and gasped. "Too thick."

The black ceiling illuminated with fluorescent green and orange streaks. One of the rock walls moved backward, exposing another tunnel. The green lights above fed into it.

He peered into the gap. The tunnel sloped downward. The strange lights in the ceiling went out.

Streak wandered into the new tunnel. "Looks safe to me."

"We'll know soon enough, won't we?"

Grey Cloak joined his dragon, and slowly they walked down the tunnel toward the torchlight illuminating the next level. Three more tunnels split off from the main passageway from where they came. One of them went straight through, and the others splintered off to the right and left at angles.

The black ceiling lit up again. Green and orange

strands of light marked the tunnels' ceilings in random patterns and vanished again. The middle tunnel's roof glowed green, and the other two turned orange and red.

"Someone's playing games with us." Grey Cloak fed more flames into the rod. "And I don't like it." He took the green tunnel. "Whoever you are, here we come."

47

A BRIGHT BLOOD-VIOLET star appeared at the top of the temple. Fog spewed from the crest and rolled down the temple, level by level, toward the bottom.

Dyphestive shook Zanna, who leaned against the structure with her eyes closed.

"Something's wrong," he said.

"Thunderbolts. That might be an understatement. We need to get Grey Cloak out of there."

He pulled his sword from the dirt. "I thought you said it wasn't very dangerous."

"It appears the legends were right, and I was wrong." She drew her short sword from the scabbard on her back. "I figured, after all this time, the temple would be dormant."

"Dormant?"

"I'll explain later." She pulled Dyphestive into the small structure.

The Red Back lizardmen blew into their horns and gathered around the temple's base. The sentries filed in from the fields surrounding the Temple Ruins, numbering in the dozens.

Dyphestive watched a pair of stout legs walk by the opening where he hid, the lizardman dragging its tail behind it. He and Zanna looked back out.

The party of Red Backs guarded the stairs that led into the temple. Others knelt on their hands and knees in worship, lifting their arms high and bowing down. The fog spewing from the temple's top covered them.

"It's going to be a fight to get inside, but we can't waste a moment," she said.

"Again, what do you mean by dormant?" he insisted.

"Most of these temples were cleaned out long ago, but the legend grows and lives on. Apparently, this temple has a new host that's using the temple as its own. The Temple Ruins are legendary for the traps and ruses that have slain countless adventurers over the decades."

"You make it sound like it has a life of its own."

"It does, perhaps," she said.

The fog crept over the grass toward them.

"We won't be able to get by them without some sort of distraction. Can I count on you?" Zanna low-crawled out of the structure. Lying on her back, she handed him a potion vial.

"What's this?"

"Fleetness. Take it and they can't catch you, but it won't last forever."

"What happens when it runs out?"

"Do what you do best. Fight." Zanna ducked and low-crawled toward the fog.

Dyphestive twisted the top off the vial and drank the substance. His blood came to life, and the veins in his arms rose. "This feels fantastic." He took his sword and walked out into the waist-deep fog. In a loud voice, Dyphestive said, "Hello, wicked foes! Would any of you like to race?"

The Red Backs broke formation, creating an opening that led right into the temple's entrance. He caught Zanna racing up the stairs and watched her vanish into the pyramid's tunnel. The Red Backs came in a rush. Dyphestive stood his ground and smiled. The Iron Sword sang.

Slice!

Steel cut through muscle and bone in the blink of an eye. Two Red Backs' bodies fell away from their waists. The other four lizardmen stopped in their tracks with their long jaws gaping.

Dyphestive didn't believe it himself. He'd struck so fast that it hadn't registered at first. He moved so fast he needed to adjust to it. He faced off with the remaining lizardmen.

Muscles bunched under their red reptilian skin. They

lowered their spears and charged. Using the full length of his long arms and two-handed sword, Dyphestive beat them to the punch. He jabbed the first two in their chests with lightning-quick thrusts and jumped back as they fell.

The last two lizardmen rushed between the fallen, head down and spears lowered, hoping to pin Dyphestive into the structure behind him. He twisted away from their spears and gored them both through their sides at the same time. In a matter of seconds, six lizardmen lay dead under the fog. More of them ran toward him. He counted.

One. Two. Four. Eight. Ten. Twelve. Sixteen. That's too many.

Dyphestive climbed on top of a stone structure and used the high ground. Spears whistled toward him. He knocked one aside with his sword and caught another.

"Anvils! I didn't see that coming." He chucked the spear into the chest of one aggressor and chopped his sword down on the other. He danced away from their spears that struck at his feet like snakes. "This is no way to fight."

With stabbing spearheads rattling off the stone beneath his feet, Dyphestive took a flying leap. He sailed over the lizardmen, landed like a deer, and sprinted toward the main temple. His long strides carried him toward the temple's base with the wind whistling by his ears.

I've never been this fast.

He climbed up the first two levels of the temple and made his way toward the top. The Red Backs chased him.

With more room to move, Dyphestive beat them down one by one. Steel bit into skull. Limbs and hands were lost. The white fog rolling down the steps turned into a blood bank. Using the fog as cover, the lizardmen lowered themselves all at once, vanishing.

Blood dripped from the tip of the Iron Sword. Dyphestive scanned the area but saw not so much as a scuffle of movement aside from the fog waterfalling past his legs. "What's the matter, fiends? Do you no longer wish to fight?" he boasted.

Stone shifted beneath his feet. He dropped down into pitch-blackness as the temple swallowed him whole.

48

"STREAK, WATCH OUT!" Grey Cloak shouted.

The ceiling above the runt dragon wobbled.

"For what?" Streak sat with his head tilted.

Grey Cloak ran, scooping up Streak a moment before a cube of ceiling came down. Stone crashed into stone. The floor trembled.

"Ah, that," Streak said. "Good call."

The temple was filled with booby traps. The falling ceiling was the fifth trap they'd evaded since entering the building.

Grey Cloak tucked Streak under his arm like a goose. "Oh no, here we go again. Pay attention." The floor cracked underneath the block of stone and spread out. The tiles in the floor began to fall away.

"Zooks!" Grey Cloak sprinted down the corridor as the

floor dropped away behind him. At the end of the tunnel, a wall of flame appeared. "This is outrageous!" He slowed. The floor dropping behind him started to catch up, opening to another bottomless pit. He covered Streak in his cloak. "Hang on. Nowhere to go but through the fire."

"You know the old saying, out of the frying pan and into the—"

Grey Cloak jumped through the flames. He landed on the other side and slid down a steep, twisting corridor on a solid sheet of ice. He kicked at the frozen ground but continued to slide like a greased pig. "Aaaaaaaah! What have I gotten myself into?"

Streak peeked out from the cloak's folds. "This is fun."

They hit a ramp and sailed over a pit.

A giant slime-covered crocodile-like monster waited for them on the other side with its jaws open wide.

"Boiling Bugsnot!" Grey Cloak spun the top of the Rod of Weapons around and fired a shot of energy down the wild beast's throat.

Bzzzt-zat!

With a roar, the monster twisted away. Grey Cloak and Streak careened into the side of its monstrous head and bounced off. The nasty creature was twice as big as them put together. Under the propulsion of its short, powerful legs, with smoke streaming from its mouth, the ugly reptilian beast charged.

"I'll handle this." Streak stood on all fours with his

wings spread. His jaws opened wide, and he spit a stream of oily flames. The fire soaked the crocodile monster's head. Its eyes burned inside their sockets. Its body and tail thrashed.

Using the Rod of Weapons like a spear, Grey Cloak took aim and jabbed it into the monster's earhole, pushing it deep. It spasmed from head to tail and moved no more. He yanked the weapon out.

Looking at the horrid creature's burning head, Streak closed his wings. "Ew. Stinky. He makes for a good light, though."

They stood inside a damp cavern with large puddles of water on the ground.

"Yes, that's exactly what I had in mind." Grey Cloak felt his heart thumping in his chest.

The flesh-and-blood monster gave him a small measure of relief. It was something he could look in the face and fight. All the other obstacles had been madness. His eyes narrowed as he surveyed the darkness. They appeared to be in a cavern underneath the temple. Piles of bones lay scattered across the rough floor along with parts of skeletons, some of them in armor and others in deteriorating robes. "This looks like the last stop for many."

Streak nodded. "You can say that again. Look at this."

Grey Cloak held his light over a skeleton dressed in rotting green wizard robes. The body lay half buried in a pile of natural rubble. A ring on one of its bony fingers caught his eye. He removed it. "It's not going to do him or her a lot of good now."

"I wonder what killed him," Streak said.

The chamber quaked.

Shards of sharp rock rained down from above.

Grey Cloak noticed busted fragments of stone all over the floor. He looked up. The ceiling was covered in a field of sharp, jagged stalactites. A large piece snapped off and dropped into the crocodile-monster's body. He picked up Streak. With no exit in sight, he kept his eyes up. He jumped away from the falling piercers that hit the ground and shattered all over.

Every direction Grey Cloak went, they fell. He danced away from crushing death like his feet were on fire. The cavern floor started to fill with them.

"This madness must end."

The piercing objects stopped falling.

"Thank goodness," he gasped.

All of a sudden, the entire sharp ceiling fell.

She'd been trapped in a stone body for decades with no feeling, no sound, no taste, left alone in the tomb of her own thoughts. It was a restless slumber without end. Now Zanna lived again. Her life's blood burned inside her body. *It's good to live again!*

Using her acute senses as a guide, she hurried into the temple, searching for any trace of Grey Cloak and Streak. In her younger days, she'd become very familiar with tombs and their traps. She understood the game. The game was death.

She looked down at the sunburst centered in the four-way intersection. A scene etched in the flames told the story. She squatted and studied it. *Interesting.*

The sunburst mural revealed a variety of booby traps spread out on every level, but they would be hard for the untrained eye to comprehend.

This is a devil of a place. But someone is running it from somewhere. The question is where? Zanna looked up at the smooth black ceiling that showed her reflection like a mirror. *Someone's watching me.*

She waved. Her image waved back, then it winked.

Oh no!

The ceiling turned into black water. The water dropped, instantly submerging her from head to toe and filling the tunnel from top to bottom. A bright light shone as the sunburst mural burned. It faded away, and Zanna's body drained into the hole.

49

DYPHESTIVE DESCENDED into blackness and hit the floor in a clamor of breaking bones. He lay flat on his back for the longest time, pain shooting through his extremities. His eyes adjusted to the darkness. A pale light from a nearby tunnel illuminated the room. He lifted a shoulder from the ground.

"Guh."

The potion's power of fleetness was gone.

Something was stuck in the back of his shoulder blades. It felt like an antler. He reached over his back and pulled it free. Bones rattled under his hands and feet. Dead bodies lay piled on the floor. The chamber reeked of rot and death.

He fought his way out of the pile of bones and grabbed

his sword lying nearby. Bony fingers seized his wrist and bit deep.

"Curse this place!" He shook off the hand and flung it aside.

The floor started to crawl. Broken bones mended. Skeletons formed and rose.

"Enough of this!" Dyphestive blasted the Iron Sword through the surging skeletons. The steel blade broke their bodies into pieces.

Frustrated beyond measure, Dyphestive went wild. He tore into the skeletons with white-eyed fury. The bony beings clawed at his limbs from all directions, dragging him into the knee-deep deteriorating flesh and bone.

Using hand and sword, he took skulls from their necks and shattered rib cages into pieces. He stomped the bones of the dead into dust. Yellow teeth bit down on his fingers. He ripped the jawbone clean out. Skeletons fell as quickly as they rose. Dyphestive annihilated them. As the bone dust settled, he stood alone.

Dragging the Iron Sword behind him, he exited the death chamber and entered into the tunnel. He only made it about twenty paces before he came face-to-face with a grid of steel bars. A wooden door waited on the other side.

"Great." He leaned his sword against the wall.

Dyphestive kicked away a skeleton that still wore chain-mail armor. One of its hands was still fastened to the bars. He spread his feet and flexed his fingers.

"I've bent thicker bars than this." He took a deep breath and grabbed them.

Bzzzzzzzzzzzt!

A jolt of searing energy spread through his limbs. His teeth rattled. He tried to let go, but his fingers were fastened to the bars. The hairs on his hand smoked. "No!"

With fire shooting through him, Dyphestive locked his jaw and grunted. He squeezed the bars and started to pull. His biceps bulged. Veins rose in his neck. He snorted like an angry bull. "Huuurk!"

The steel began to bend to the will of his rock-hard iron muscle. Metal groaned, spit, and sizzled. The grid ripped open like torn fabric. The shock and agonizing energy flowing through it disappeared.

With his smoking hair standing on end, Dyphestive pushed the metal, rolling it back and out of the way. He picked up his sword and squeezed through. Using his index finger, he touched the metal handle on the door beyond. It didn't shock him.

"Whew. It's time to get out of here."

He grabbed the handle, pushed the thumb lever down, and pulled the door open wide. He stepped through. The floor plate beneath him clicked.

Anvils!

Javelins shot out of the small holes in the walls and pinned him through the belly and chest.

Water flooded the pit in the center of the temple. Zanna fell into it. The foamy surge splashed down on her like a waterfall, holding her under. She held her breath, swimming in the blackness with water crashing on her head. The flow came to a stop, and she treaded water in total darkness.

The floor above her with the mosaic sunburst sealed her in the deep. Its fiery outline glowed with the sun staring at her, a cruel smile playing on its lips.

Zanna would have to tread water or drown. Her own weapons and gear pulled her down.

The water buzzed to life beneath her.

"Now what?"

A small fish swam by her nose. Something nipped at her belly. She felt it bite through the skin and draw blood. Piranhas swarmed her. The waters stirred, bubbling on the surface.

"Oh no, you don't! I'm not going to die bit by bit." She summoned her wizardry. The magic inside her caught fire. She closed her eyes and sent a hot blast out of her body.

Pooomph!

Hundreds of dead fish floated to the surface, creating a blanket of scales on top of the water.

"Nasty." Zora swam through it to the far wall. She'd dealt with such traps before. Her fingers dusted over the stone wall's smooth surface. In the darkness, she found small finger- and toeholds. She climbed out of the water and scaled the wall like a spider.

The face inside the sunburst frowned. Its glow brightened. The pit heated up.

With her jaw set, Zanna climbed toward the skin-boiling heat. The hot air grew suffocating. She inched farther up and didn't stop until she was a few feet from the top. Her skin burned.

She drew her short sword from her back, filled it with wizard fire, and stared down the sun. "If I go, you go!" She stabbed it.

A bright white light flashed.

Coughing and kicking, Grey Cloak fought his way out of the pile of smothering, rocky debris. The Cloak of Legends had shielded him from the piercing tips of the stalactites, and the ceiling above was empty.

"How do you fare, Streak?" he asked the dragon cradled against his body.

"Doing well. What do you say we find a way out of here?" Streak shook the dust off his scales like a hound shedding water. "I mean, how much worse can it be?"

"Agreed." Grey Cloak flapped his cloak. In the next instant, his body was bathed in bright light. "Streeeeeeak!"

50

Grey Cloak rubbed the purple spots inside his eyelids. He swayed, caught his balance, and opened his eyes. Another white light flashed beside him.

Zanna appeared, sword in hand, soaked head to toe in water. She slung her hair out of her face. "You live. Good."

They were inside a square chamber where the four walls slanted down and away from them. Grey Cloak immediately thought he was inside one of the top levels of the temple. As his eyes cleared, he saw a strange-looking person sitting on a stone throne. A chill ran down his spine.

"What in the—"

The chamber washed a vivid white. He shielded his eyes and blinked the spots away. Dyphestive stood beside him. A javelin protruded from his side.

"Brother!" Grey Cloak said, alarmed.

Dyphestive had deep piercings in his torso and superficial scratch wounds all over. He looked like he'd run through a briar patch with more briars than patch.

"What happened?"

"I don't know where to start." Dyphestive looked at the javelin sticking out of his front and back. "Horseshoes, I missed one."

"I am the Temple Master," the figure said in an eerie alien voice.

Grey Cloak turned his attention to the person sitting in the great chair.

The Temple Master had a small body like a gnome or halfling. His skin was a pale purple, filled with blue veins. Bare-chested, he wore only a ceremonial dress. It was the only normal thing about the strange person. His large, spacey eyes bulged in their sockets, and he had no eyelids. His face was twice the size of his body, and no skull covered his brain. In place of a skull, his transparent skin revealed all the impressions of his gray matter.

The Temple Master continued. "You are formidable, true survivors, proven. I will let you take one possession, then you must take your leave."

Grey Cloak noticed Streak was missing. "I want my dragon back."

"The lizard?" The Temple Master's eyes rolled into his head and shuddered back and forth. "I don't see him." He passed his hand through the air.

Panels in the rock wall became living pictures inside the temple. They could see the rooms they had passed through, the tunnels leading in and out. It showed images of the world outside. The illustrations covered the room.

Temple Master tapped his fingers together. "I have been entertained. Take one article of treasure, and take your leave. I insist."

A table appeared between them and the Temple Master. It stretched from one side of the room to the other and held small treasure boxes, well-crafted ancient weapons of all sorts, rings, brooches, amulets, wands, staffs, and unique garments.

"Take one for you all," the Temple Master said.

Grey Cloak spotted a smooth river stone about the size of a man's head. It had a crude face in the middle, and the sides flared up like wings. A rudimentary paint job made it look like a dragon.

Dyphestive picked it up. "I believe this is what we came for."

"How disappointing," Grey Cloak said.

The Temple Master looked puzzled. "A poor choice."

"That's a matter of opinion," Grey Cloak said. "Now, where's my dragon?"

"Your lizard is no concern of mine. Be happy you live." The Temple Master blinked.

Grey Cloak, Dyphestive, and Zanna reappeared outside, staring up at the bright eye illuminating the top of the temple. The fog had cleared, and dead Red Backs lay everywhere.

"I'm going back in." Grey Cloak started toward the stairs, but the entire pyramid quaked.

Using the ceilings like a hallway, Streak moseyed through the temple. Like a small lizard, his little talons had no trouble clinging to the surface. His tongue flickered out of his mouth, and he caught the scent of his friends inside a network of smaller tunnels underneath the floors and between the walls and ceilings. Though the space was far too small for a person to wiggle through, Streak had no trouble navigating it. He moved toward the top of the temple.

He popped his head out of the ancient aperture, where he heard voices. Grey Cloak, Dyphestive, and Zanna spoke to an alien person with more head than body. He peeked down from his spot on the ceiling, listening to the conversation. A white flash blinded Streak momentarily. His second eyelids that shielded his eyes rose, renewing his focus instantly. His friends were gone.

The Temple Master laughed wickedly. "Ah-hahahaha. No one enters my temple and lives to tell about it."

The images on the wall started to change. One of the larger images showed the heroes standing outside in the field. The rest of the images were inside the temple. Walls opened, and scores of grotesque gargoyles stepped out.

"Gargoyle army, seek out the living flesh and blood, and do not return until you've destroyed them." The Temple Master made a clicking sound. "Death and destruction is so very entertaining."

Streak looked straight down on the Temple Master's head. "Hey, Big Brain, you forgot someone."

"You! The lizard! How did you find me?"

Streak dropped down on top of the Temple Master's cushiony head and sank his claws in deep. "Let's just say I have a nose for finding trouble."

"Get off my head!"

"As you wish, but first..." Streak unleashed a breath, setting the Temple Master's head on fire. He put it all into the fire and jumped back to the ceiling.

"Noooo! Noooo!" The Temple Master ran back and forth across the room, wildly waving his arms, trying to reach up and pat out the flames eating away at his brain.

The images on the walls flashed in and out in sporadic patterns. The temple walls flexed and bowed, then began to collapse.

"I'd love to stick around." Streak crawled back into the ancient aperture. "But you look kinda busy. And, Big Brain, call me."

The temple collapsed from top to bottom, level by level coming down. The great eye above it winked out. The Red Back lizardmen that had survived the battle with Dyphestive took off running. The trio of heroes backpedaled. Rock came down on rock with explosive sounds.

BOOM! BOOM! BOOM-BOOM-BOOM!

A brown cloud rolled over the fields, coating everything in rock dust.

As the smoke cleared, Grey Cloak hollered, "Streak! Streak!"

Silence fell over the valley of the Temple Ruins. Even the crickets quieted.

Streak materialized out of the dust cloud and appeared high in the sky. "Chalk one up to the Streak-meister. Big Brain has been defeated."

After removing the javelin from his body, Dyphestive returned the idol to Keena and Bosco the Mender. Bosco could barely hold the heavy natural sculpture in his arms.

He dropped it on the ground. "Eh, it's too heavy. Did you happen to see something similar but smaller that we could use?"

Grey Cloak gave Zanna a look. "Don't say it. I'll say it for you. I told you so."

51

THE PRESENT

TALON RODE out of the Green Ridges into the bitter landscape of a dry and dusty land. The journey was long and hard, and the conversation sparse. Ahead, a mirage-like image of a city nestled underneath the blazing sun, its back to the shadows of the rocky mountains cradling it from behind.

Crane took a deep breath and put a friendly smile on his face. "Welcome to Farstick. It's as close to nowhere as you could ever hope to be."

What does the future hold for our heroes?

Can they survive the coming trials at the Flaming Fence?

How long can Grey Cloak and Dyphestive remain hidden from the allies of Black Frost?

Find out in Book #16 - BEDLAM. On sale now! Click this link or cover below!

And don't forget to leave a review on Book 15: LINK

You can learn more about the strange world of Barton and the Arachnamen in the Darkslayer Omnibus. On Sale Now!

LINK

And if you haven't already, signup for my newsletter and grab 3 FREE books including the Dragon Wars Prequel.

WWW.DRAGONWARSBOOKS.COM

Teachers and Students, if you would like to order paperback copies for you library or classroom, email craig@thedarkslayer.com to receive a special discount.

Gear up in this Dragon Wars body armor enchanted with a +2 Coolness factor/+4 at Gaming Conventions. Sizes range from halfling (Small) to Ogre (XXL). LINK . www.society6.com

ABOUT THE AUTHOR

*Check me out on Bookbub and follow: HalloranOn-BookBub

*I'd love it if you would subscribe to my mailing list: www.craighalloran.com

*On Facebook, you can find me at The Darkslayer Report or Craig Halloran.

*Twitter, Twitter, Twitter. I am there, too: www.twitter.com/CraigHalloran

*And of course, you can always email me at craig@thedarkslayer.com

See my book lists below!

OTHER BOOKS

Craig Halloran resides with his family outside his hometown of Charleston, West Virginia. When he isn't entertaining mankind, he is seeking adventure, working out, or watching sports. To learn more about him, go to www.thedarkslayer.com.

Check out all my great stories...

Free Books

The Red Citadel and the Sorcerer's Power

The Darkslayer: Brutal Beginnings

Nath Dragon—Quest for the Thunderstone

The Chronicles of Dragon Series 1 (10-book series)

The Hero, the Sword and the Dragons (Book 1)

Dragon Bones and Tombstones (Book 2)

Terror at the Temple (Book 3)

Clutch of the Cleric (Book 4)

Hunt for the Hero (Book 5)

Siege at the Settlements (Book 6)

Strife in the Sky (Book 7)

Fight and the Fury (Book 8)

War in the Winds (Book 9)

Finale (Book 10)

Boxset 1-5

Boxset 6-10

Collector's Edition 1-10

Tail of the Dragon, The Chronicles of Dragon, Series 2 (10-book series)

Tail of the Dragon #1

Claws of the Dragon #2

Battle of the Dragon #3

Eyes of the Dragon #4

Flight of the Dragon #5

Trial of the Dragon #6

Judgement of the Dragon #7

Wrath of the Dragon #8

Power of the Dragon #9

Hour of the Dragon #10

Boxset 1-5

Boxset 6-10

Collector's Edition 1-10

<u>**The Odyssey of Nath Dragon Series (New Series) (Prequel to Chronicles of Dragon)**</u>

Exiled

Enslaved

Deadly

Hunted

Strife

<u>**The Darkslayer Series 1 (6-book series)**</u>

Wrath of the Royals (Book 1)

Blades in the Night (Book 2)

Underling Revenge (Book 3)

Danger and the Druid (Book 4)

Outrage in the Outlands (Book 5)

Chaos at the Castle (Book 6)

Boxset 1-3

Boxset 4-6

Omnibus 1-6

<u>**The Darkslayer: Bish and Bone, Series 2 (10-book series)**</u>

Bish and Bone (Book 1)

Black Blood (Book 2)

Red Death (Book 3)

Lethal Liaisons (Book 4)

Torment and Terror (Book 5)

Brigands and Badlands (Book 6)
War in the Wasteland (Book 7)
Slaughter in the Streets (Book 8)
Hunt of the Beast (Book 9)
The Battle for Bone (Book 10)
Boxset 1-5
Boxset 6-10
Bish and Bone Omnibus (Books 1-10)

CLASH OF HEROES: Nath Dragon meets The Darkslayer mini series

Book 1
Book 2
Book 3

The Henchmen Chronicles

The King's Henchmen
The King's Assassin
The King's Prisoner
The King's Conjurer
The King's Enemies
The King's Spies

The Gamma Earth Cycle

Escape from the Dominion
Flight from the Dominion
Prison of the Dominion

The Supernatural Bounty Hunter Files (10-book series)

Smoke Rising: Book 1

I Smell Smoke: Book 2

Where There's Smoke: Book 3

Smoke on the Water: Book 4

Smoke and Mirrors: Book 5

Up in Smoke: Book 6

Smoke Signals: Book 7

Holy Smoke: Book 8

Smoke Happens: Book 9

Smoke Out: Book 10

Boxset 1-5

Boxset 6-10

Collector's Edition 1-10

Zombie Impact Series

Zombie Day Care: Book 1

Zombie Rehab: Book 2

Zombie Warfare: Book 3

Boxset: Books 1-3

OTHER WORKS & NOVELLAS

The Red Citadel and the Sorcerer's Power

Made in the USA
Monee, IL
23 June 2021